I0772965

In Karen Lee's powerful memoir, "'The Village that Betrayed its Children," she delves into the themes of secrecy, denial, and shame surrounding the trauma of child sexual abuse. Through her narrative, Lee vividly illustrates the creation and lasting repercussions of the unseen wounds that persist "hidden, unacknowledged, and unhealed" from bullying, abuse, and neglect.

Young children, betrayed by their teacher and disavowed by the very adults meant to shield them, were left to endure and to protect themselves from the monster in their midst. It is a story that illuminates the profound impact of abuse. Lee's memoir poignantly portrays the lifelong physical and psychological impacts of childhood sexual abuse: anxiety, depression, low self-esteem, withdrawal, grief, and addiction, all exacerbated by the absence of reparative justice. She lays bare the reality of how such abuse forever altered her life, and the lives of many of her former classmates, leaving behind a legacy of pain, anger, shattered relationships, and inner turmoil. Vulnerability became a shield, as victims retreated into guilt and silence, leaving wounds, great and small, that festered over the course of their lives.

Lee's narrative unfolds with raw emotion, revealing the shock, humiliation, and anger that permeate the survivors' experiences. Through Lee's courageous storytelling, readers come to grasp how the hidden pain of the past manifests in the present, urging us toward a collective reckoning and a path forward.

Nancy Ogden, PhD, Chair, Department of Psychology,
Professor, Psychology,
Mount Royal University, Calgary Alberta

I got lost in Karen Lee's story. Half a century later, Karen shares a real and raw pain she was not supposed to share. Rather, the little girl was to keep quiet and let The Teacher, a known pedophile, molest her and other little girls.
It was the worse kept secret. Living a hoot and a holler from Leskard, I heard the rumours.
The author's parents, neighbours, school board, police, doctors and church, failed her.
It was an absolute injustice.

Joan Ransberry was raised a stone's throw from Leskard, is a Graduate of journalism from Durham College, Oshawa, Ontario, and a former Torstar reporter with 35 years in the media.

The Village That Betrayed Its Children

A Memoir

By
Karen Elizabeth Lee

AOS PUBLISHING, 2024

ISBN: 978-1-990496-71-4

Cover Design: Chanelle Poupart

Visit AOS Publishing's website:
www.aospublishing.com

Acknowledgements

Thank you to those I interviewed and who gave generously of their time and interest to this project:

Carole Grant Anderson
Brian Buckley,
Joy Ball,
Marilyn Cobbledick Barraball
Ruth Chater,
Beryl Clarke
Anita DeVries
Ken Frame
Randy Flynn
Clifford Francis
Joan Gimblett,
Shelley Battams Gifford
David Green
Cathy Spry Haick
Donna Hart
Philip Loucks
Joan Ransberry
Helen Schmidt

My sincere thanks to Kevin, Elsii, and Kaiya, the present owners of the Hive in Leskard, the staff at the Clarington Museum in Bowmanville, and those people who supported me in this endeavour, both directly and indirectly, including Jenny McDonnel, Rick Beaver, Julie Ireton, Renos Papadopoulos, Anne Petrie, Jason Lee, Rachel Lee, David Cozens, Denise Snyder, Jane Pollard, Liz Kozub Nascimben, Mary Spensley, Melody Bundt, Nancy Ogden, Peta Heskell, Lauren Carter, Rosemary Griebel, my loving husband, Bill Guse, who did the initial reading of the manuscript, my sons and daughters-in-law and grandsons.

If there are errors in memory, the errors are all mine.

This book is dedicated to all who went to Leskard School during this terrible time in its history, and particularly to Joy Ball who said, "Thank you, Karen. I cried through reading your manuscript. Maybe I can get a healing now."

To all of us who need healing.

Table of Contents

Bad men need nothing more to compass their ends, than
that good men should look on and do nothing.

— John Stuart Mill, 1867

Chapter 1
He's Still Alive

David had my Teacher's hands. This ordinary man had my Teacher's hands. Fat and white, pudgy and doughy fingers, like the ones on my Teacher's hands. Those hands were attached to the body of an otherwise normal man. Sticking out of his sleeves.

But let me back up a little. In September 1998, I flew to Prague to conduct a training program for a medical company with David, a consultant I'd never worked with before. I met him in our hotel lobby and we walked to a lovely rooftop restaurant in the old town, near Wenceslas Square, and next to the Vltava River, so we could get to know one another and go over the project.

While we talked, I couldn't pay attention. I was following David's every hand movement as he picked up his knife, cut his meat, and carried each piece with his fork to his mouth. An uneasiness crept over me.

The next morning, before the participants arrived at the course location, we began discussing icebreaker exercises to begin the workshop. As though possessed, I answered in a scathing, sarcastic tone, "I'm not going to do *that* exercise. You can just think of something else." I raised my voice, repeatedly criticizing this perfectly reasonable man who had done nothing wrong—and watched the growing alarm and dislike on his face. A cold fear came over me, as I slowly realized what I had done and why.

I confessed, "I'm so sorry. Your hands remind me of someone, of something that happened a long time ago."

David turned away in a sharp motion that told me everything. He must have thought I was crazy.

"Please," I said, almost begging. "It isn't anything you've done."

But he didn't want to talk to me, and frankly, there was no good way to explain to a stranger that he had the same hands as a pedophile. What could I say?

I'd never understood why I had an obsession for looking at men's hands. But that morning something clicked into place, like that last piece of a jigsaw puzzle you need to complete the picture. When I met a man, any man, I looked at his hands almost before saying hello. I'd been watching out for my Teacher's hands.

I thought my past was locked down tight, but it wasn't. I thought if I avoided the village where I'd grown up, I wouldn't be haunted. But there, thousands of miles from my childhood home, my Teacher had sprung out of the past with no warning. Almost as though he were still alive.

Chapter 2
Going Home

During my growing-up years, I'd been nervous of my parents, the house we lived in, the village and the countryside. As an adult, I was still frightened of what I would discover if I looked too closely into the turmoil of what had happened all those years ago.

I'd held myself apart from village life for so long, I'd become an outsider, a tourist, even. Perhaps I thought I could escape, could run away, yet both the future and past haunted me in my dreams. In one dream, *my father was terminally ill. I was angry, and challenged my Mother, "How do you think it feels for me to be so far away, always missing everyone's birthdays and weddings? Doesn't anyone realize how much I care?"* My dreams were showing me what I could barely admit to myself—I'd paid a high price for my fear of the village and my discomfort around my parents.

But all these many years later, I needed to know the truth about the Teacher, our village, why it had all been allowed to happen. I had to go back.

I knew I had to face what had happened all those years ago—and I knew it wasn't going to be easy. First, it had happened over sixty years ago. I would have to sort through memories, the fragments of stories, the rumours, the documents. Finding out and telling others' experiences would fill gaps in my own story, and help me see the world through the villagers' and my former classmates' eyes. I would have to locate and talk with those who used to live in Leskard, those who were still alive. The second consideration was the painful emotions I would finally have to face from my childhood, both inside and outside the school.

In the spring of 2018, three years after my mother died, and many years after my father had died, our old family home in the country had been sold and so was no longer ours. If I were to go back to Ontario to find out about my past, I had to find a place to stay. I wanted to rent a room in the village or as close to it as I could. One hundred years before, there had been a hotel next to the general store—but it was long gone by 1957, when my family had moved to Leskard, Ontario. After an online search, I found a B&B in the village called The Hive—in the old village church. I sent them an email.

The rooms were fully booked. I was so disappointed, I wrote back to the B&B owners, Elsii and Kevin, and explained that I was a former village resident coming to do local research. They immediately wrote back and said they could fit me in—if I didn't mind staying in the church.

I imagined the church as I had known it as a child—with the school next to it. I was unnerved by the possibility that I might be that close to the school, so I looked up The Hive on Google Maps. I was glad I did, because the map showed a house, now part of the B&B, in the small field that used to separate the church and the school. I wouldn't be able to see the school from the church.

The closer it got to the date of the trip, the more anxious I felt. Years before, while I was writing a memoir about my two disastrous marriages, I had unwittingly signalled to my brain that I was going to delve into the past. Dreams, thoughts, and whole imagined scenes had intruded on my life. I knew I might be risking that again. But this time, the taboo against lifting the rock off this part of my past seemed even more daunting. I felt I would be defying the whole village and my late parents.

* * *

I made a reservation for a return flight from Calgary to Toronto—which I'd done every couple of months from 2010 to 2015 while my mother had been in a Port Hope nursing home. But it was different since Mom had died. I was no longer wondering what condition she'd be in when I arrived, what problems I'd have to sort out with the banks and healthcare professionals, and what relatives I'd have to deal with. This time I had no concerns but my project.

The story of the Teacher and what he did in my elementary school had never been made public, so I pondered a number of things. Did this story have to be told, or should it remain hidden? Was it up to me to write the story—because I knew I was not the only one he affected. Possibly it was falling on me simply because of the pain I still carried with me, and my anger that it had all been allowed to happen.

I landed in Toronto and picked up a rental car. I drove north out of the spaghetti freeway exit from the airport, onto Highway 27 and exited onto the 407 East. The 407 is a toll road, which entails a cost, but it saves on the nervous exhaustion that comes with driving through Toronto on the twelve-lane 401 lined with high-rises. Instead, once you drive east, north of Scarborough, the 407 wends its way through fields and small-town Ontario. I could breathe. I was home. I drove through the tiny town of Brooklin, up and down hills, and around sharp turns on the back-country road that led to the village of Tyrone, where my brother lives.

Tyrone, named after County Tyrone in Ireland, has changed little in appearance since it was settled well over two hundred years ago, though now the school, corner general store, and blacksmith shop have closed. The old two-storey grain mill, built in 1846, with its grey wood clapboard and white multi-paned windows, sitting on the edge of the old mill pond, still looks the same, but has found new life as an outlet for fresh produce, cheeses, home-baked bread, donuts, and pies.

Just beyond the mill is my brother's house. I pulled into his driveway to say hi to him, as I did every time I came home. After a brief catch-up, I told him I was going to stay in a B&B in Leskard, and wanted to find out more about Mr. Pollard, our old Principal and Teacher, so I could write my story. My brother is nine years younger than me, so was never in Mr. Pollard's classroom. The new regional school was built and he went there after Pollard briefly left the area.

My brother looked worried and barked, "But you can't name him!"

I reassured him that writing about people who have died was permitted, but he wasn't convinced. However, he also didn't realize that my considering the past would lead me to question our parents' decisions all those years ago. We planned to meet later in Bowmanville for supper and I drove on toward Leskard, about four miles east of Tyrone.

The road from my brother's house to Leskard runs right past our childhood home. As I approached our old house, I slowed, then stopped on the side of the road. My heart filled with heavy sadness, love, and some underlying resentment that this place was no longer ours. I was not going to pull into the long driveway lined with century-old spruce trees. It was sold in 2014, a year before our mother passed away, a decision that still goes round and round in my head, like fingers endlessly clicking rosary beads. I sat in the car and remembered.

Chapter 3
The Church Meeting
Where I Announce My Intention

I brought myself back from my reveries in front of our old house, put the car into drive, and moved on, descending two hills to the village corner and then driving partway up the next hill. I pulled in beside The Hive, the B&B located in the old Leskard United church, and got out of my car to meet the owners and my hosts.

On the outside, the church looked as I remembered it: built in 1850, red brick, with a dark-wood, double-front door topped with a pointed window framed in white, and tall pointy-topped windows on either side. A set of stairs led up to the front door, but now the cement was covered in a cladding of stone. I went to the back door and knocked.

My hosts welcomed me in. Elsii and Kevin were relative newcomers to Leskard—they had only lived in the village for eighteen years. Kevin had long dark hair tied at the back, Elsii was dressed simply in a flower-printed cotton dress— and they were vegetarians. The food at the strawberry suppers held long ago in the church annex might have been natural, even organic, but I never heard those words in the 1950s.

The pews and pulpit were gone. White walls and polished pine floors were the background for the antiques that filled every corner of the church's large open space, including shiny dark wood tables banked with pressed-back chairs. The kitchen took up the back left-hand corner of the room.

They showed me up the wooden staircase to a mezzanine level, off which a hallway led to the back of the church. I was given the last room, looking out over the grass and wooded area at the back. It was decorated with white lace on the bedspread and pillows, an antique dresser, baskets filled with fluffy towels, and hand-made bars of perfumed soaps. B&B décor had come to Leskard. Perhaps I had been away too long.

Kevin and Elsii knew little of the village's history—nothing of the school and the Teacher. But they were interested in the project I'd initially said was a history of the village. They'd sent out invitations to people in the area asking them to come for lunch and to share stories.

After I'd unpacked a few things, changed my clothes, and brushed my teeth, I wandered the village, going down the road I used to walk before and after school each day. I tried to remember the families that had lived in each house. The one across the road from the church was undergoing some sort of reconstruction—it had been the Gimblett family home. Up the hill, on the same side, was the house Ken Frame lived in—whose children had gone to Leskard School. On the next corner down the hill was the Martins' house, where Alan Martin had lived. A new house had been built west of the church where an old classmate, and his wife, now lived.

The old general store that stood at the corner where Leskard Road meets the 8th Concession had been renovated by descendants of the Gerrows, the last family to run the store. Instead of facing the main intersection of the village, as it had for over one hundred years, it was now a house with the main door opening to the side. Little was left of the original storefront.

Along Leskard Road, I could see some of my old classmates' homes— the Green family's, the house where Marilyn Eade had lived, the Thompsons' house and the large white clapboard house where my sister's best friend had lived. Brian Buckley, a bit younger than me, still lived in the village, in his great aunt Jennie's old house, and nearby, Ruth Chater still lived on the Chater family farm.

The valley where the village stands is filled with dark looming cedars, tall maple trees, trout creeks, remnants of old mill ponds, historic homes interwoven with new homes. But I hadn't been able to stay. I'd wanted to get out as fast as I could and hadn't wanted to go into the village or reconnect with village people. I felt apart and wanted to stay apart. But I never told my parents any of this. The reasons. We just didn't talk about things like that—nothing that was important.

* * *

The following day, I stood in the large open space of the church, paced, and looked around while I waited for the luncheon to begin. Jill, one of my former school playmates, walked in the back door with her older brother, but at first I didn't recognize her. She came up to me and said, "Hi, do you remember me?" And, while she was definitely familiar, she had changed so much, it took a minute or so before I saw my old friend in this stylish older woman. Her brother said he remembered me battling up the hill in the wind and snow after he, his brothers, and sister turned up their road to go home.

Peggy Sutcliffe came up to me and said, "Remember making those root beer floats and popcorn when I came to babysit you?" Decades before, both she and her sister had babysat me, my sister, and brother. I hadn't seen them since.

Marilyn Barraball, who'd taught my younger sister and brother, had been the Junior room teacher when she was Miss Cobbledick. She looked trim and remarkably young—yet she had to be close to eighty. Then Ken Frame arrived, bringing photos and maps.

The B&B hosts had put out sliced meats, cheeses, and bread so the guests could make themselves sandwiches, coffee, and dessert to enjoy while we discussed old memories.

I looked at the white hair and aged faces of those I'd known in the village and gone to elementary school with, and noticed a disconnect. I had missed all the intervening years during which we'd all finished school, worked, and had our children. For me, they were all suddenly older... decades older. My eyes misted over when I realized how I'd avoided these people all these long years, knowing it had nothing to do with them.

I stood in front of the group, trembling slightly, and hoped that, when I shared the real reason I had wanted to meet, they wouldn't feel they'd been invited under false pretenses.

I began, "Thank you for coming today. I am so pleased to see you all here. This valley and the village are so beautiful and yet, when I left to go to university, I didn't want to come back." I paused, nervous, fearful that if I mentioned the past, someone would challenge me with, "Why do you have to bring all that up?" or "That was so long ago; it doesn't matter now," or "Just get over it."

I continued, "I had such a difficult time here at the school. The village was faced with something it couldn't deal with and didn't want to deal with." *I saw nods and heard whispers.* Then I stated, "I was molested by the Teacher."

As soon as I said this, two women put up their hands simultaneously and said, "Me, too."

I was astonished—if two, three counting me, in this tiny gathering, had been molested, how many more were there?

One man shouted out, "No young girls were safe with the Teacher!" If he knew, how many others were aware of what had happened?

I continued, "The village was a combination of innocence and denial and the only perpetrator was the Teacher." *I didn't want to point fingers, to have anyone feel responsible—even deceased village residents.*

The former Junior teacher looked stunned. Later, she and I were able to talk.

"I heard rumours at the time from relatives who lived in the area. I went to my teaching mentor and she told me I had to witness wrong-doing by Mr. Pollard or I couldn't do anything—and neither could she."

More information I didn't know. I said, trying to smooth over the awkwardness, "Yes, that's how things were back then—no one really wanted to deal with things out of their comfort zone, or risk making mistakes."

But, though I tried not to be judgmental, I ached inside with sadness. Possibly someone could have saved us, all those years ago.

When we were finished eating and chatting, several of us exchanged email addresses and phone numbers and promised to stay in touch. I made arrangements to meet Jill for lunch the next day.

I did place the blame firmly on the Teacher for his behaviour, but I wanted more—I wanted to find out how the village had allowed evil to be brought onto the children. Who knew what was happening? How many did he touch? I knew my journey would be hard, but it had to be done. I am over seventy, so if I don't look into this now, who will—and when?

Chapter 4
Research At The Clarington Museum

The next morning, I enjoyed breakfast with Kevin and Elsii, then drove to the Clarington Museum in Bowmanville. I'd already phoned for an appointment to go through the archives of our village, and our school. When I arrived, there were two carts loaded with files to look at.

However, though the staff was helpful, the museum only contained records and artifacts given by donation, so there was an incomplete collection of local documents. Some Leskard School ledgers were in the archives, but a note indicated that the more recent records had been placed in the vault in the old elementary school in Orono, and then moved to the Kawartha Pine Ridge District School board offices in Peterborough. A subsequent phone call to Peterborough indicated no one knew where they were.

Later, in a phone interview with Randy Flynn, who'd had Mr. Pollard as his grade five teacher, I learned how some ledgers had ended up in the museum. After our school in Leskard was closed in 1966 and before it was sold and turned into a private home, Randy and another child went into the empty building. They found several documents, including the large old attendance ledgers. They took them home and their parents gave them to the Clarke Township Museum located, at that time, in the old Kirby village school, just off Highway 115 and north of Concession 7. Then they were donated to the Clarington Museum, where I saw them.

I placed one of the huge teachers' ledgers for S.S. # 15, Clarke (Leskard) on the museum table and opened it. The entries started in the 1930s and ended in 1956, the year before I'd moved to Leskard. I wasn't there. I wanted to be there. I wanted this ledger to confirm I'd gone to Leskard school when the Teacher was teaching.

The names of some of the children I'd gone to school with were listed—Jill and her brothers, Marilyn Eade, the Thompsons, the Buckleys, Alex and Burt Green who had lived on the farm next to us when we moved to Leskard, Alan Martin, the Loucks children. I learned the names of other teachers, including Jill's mother, who had taught there for one year.

I also learned that the Teacher himself, long before he was the Principal and Teacher, had been a pupil at Leskard Public School, had transferred to Oak school further east on the eighth line for a year, and then returned to finish grade eight in Leskard. Because he grew up north of the village on the 9th concession, on the Pollard family farm, I should have realized he must have gone to school in Leskard, but I had moved there when I was eight and, like many children, never thought of any teacher having a life outside the classroom. He wasn't a person, he was the Teacher.

Everything in the ledger was hand-written. I recognized the Teacher's handwriting immediately. I still have some of my handwritten report cards at home—saved by my mother. I reached my fingers out to the ledger and touched the place where he had written the children's names, the girls' names. I shivered, looked away from the book, and then looked again. I wanted answers, but they weren't on these pages.

After I set aside the school ledgers, I looked at some of the original photos of my village, the houses, the general store, the school, the wooden bridge that used to go over

Wilmot Creek, and the road up to the school, that had all been used in the book *Out of the Mists*, by authors Helen Schmid, a local historian, and Sid Rutherford, my former high school vice-principal. Also, there were their original typed chapters.

When I had started my research at home, I found family photos my parents had saved and pictures of our village, the school, the old store, local houses, and roads. *Out of the Mists*, a history of our township, Clarke Township, sat on my bookshelf. I had gone to this book for information about the village from the time it was founded. I'd also looked online for the Teacher and found a picture of his headstone, the names of his parents, the dates of his birth and death.

I hadn't anticipated seeing any displays at the museum that would add to my research into the Teacher, the school, and the village, but the current exhibit featured huge photos and some history of the Bowmanville Training School, built in 1925 just east of the village of Bowmanville.

The display concentrated on the time the Training School was Camp 30, a World War Two prisoner of war camp that housed about eight hundred high-ranking Nazi officers captured by the Allies. After the war ended, the camp was returned to its original purpose, the rehabilitation of young boys, only to be closed in 1984.

It was meant to be the most progressive training school in Canada—a place to send boys aged eight to fourteen to be "reformed." Hundreds of Ontario boys, considered wayward, or just a burden to their parents, were sent by the courts to do time at the training school. But the display didn't contain the history of its years as a training school, nor anything about the children who spent time there. It said nothing about Billy Churchill, a boy who'd been incarcerated there during the fifties and trained to be a farm worker. He'd attended Leskard school, and played a role in engendering my fear of the Teacher and the village.

Though not part of my original plan, after finishing at the museum, I decided to drive to the training school property on the east side of Bowmanville. I parked on Lambs Road, which runs to the east of the site, and walked across the road. The grounds were overgrown with grass and weeds, but some of the paved paths were still intact. I tried to imagine the boys who had lived there, "see" them walking on the sidewalks. Buildings, or what remained of them, were covered with graffiti, the windows smashed, their bowels laid open to show where fires had been lit and broken glass had littered the floors. I turned and ran back to my car, opened the door, sat in the driver's seat, and locked myself in.

I knew I would have to come back to the story of Billy Churchill to fully tell the story of my village, the school, and the Teacher. But for now, I breathed heavily, turned the key, and drove back to Leskard and the B&B.

* * *

After the meeting at the B&B and the research at the museum, I flew back to Calgary. Though overwhelmed with what I'd learned and at the enormity of the project facing me, my need to know the truth, to understand what had happened, drove me forward.

First, I emailed those who'd attended the B&B lunch to establish connections and ask them for more stories and insights into our village. Interestingly, one of the women who had declared "me, too" when I said I'd been molested, didn't reply. I recognized that some people were still reluctant to talk about it, despite all the intervening years. One man's wife simply didn't want them to get involved, and another didn't want to be in my manuscript.

I posted a message on several Facebook town sites local to my old village asking anyone with information to contact me. People emailed me with stories—some had also been victimized, some had witnessed abuse, others had heard rumours, and some speculated about why nothing had been done. Even people outside the village had heard about the Teacher. I set up online and phone interviews with former classmates. I hoped that by digging into the past, I would learn why and how it had happened—and how it affected us all. The truth.

I would have to explore what others had to say about the Teacher, but I also knew I'd have to look at my parents and their decision to send my sister and I back to the school. I wanted to understand how people could do this, knowing the Teacher was a molester of young girls.

So, why was finding the truth *my* job? I had let my experience with the Teacher drive me, haunt me, define me, affect my mental health—I didn't know who I was without this experience. I needed some sort of peace for myself.

Also, it wasn't just my parents' deaths that allowed me to delve into this now. My life experiences and training as a psychologist had given me a different perspective on what had happened. When I was young, I automatically didn't confront my mother or my father—I didn't even consider it. But when Mom was sick, old, frail, I didn't want the conflict—for her sake or mine. Though I returned home, month after month, year after year, to help her through her illness, fearing her reactions, I still hadn't asked her some important questions. Now I'd have to rely on others to give me some of the answers I needed.

Chapter 5
My Mother's Illness

When I was a child, my relationship with my mother had been difficult—and it hadn't gotten any better as I'd grown older. After I was widowed at the age of fifty, she regularly phoned to talk about crazy political stories, to ask if I was promiscuous, to discourage me from seeing certain men who, in her mind, were womanizers, or to ridicule my dress sense. If I countered her fears and assertions with facts, she simply slammed down the phone. Yet she still wanted to visit me. She didn't see herself as difficult. But, in the summer of 2010, when I'd picked up the phone back in Calgary, she wasn't angry. She was upset.

Mom told me she had fainted in the Loblaws grocery store at the Oshawa Centre mall. The store officials had called an ambulance to take her to the Oshawa Hospital.

"Mom, what's wrong, what do they say is wrong?" I leaned back on my kitchen counter as I listened to the story.

"I have blood cancer. I have to go to Toronto, to St. Michaels, a hospital in Toronto. They are going to send me there, take out all my blood, and put back clean blood. Then I'll be fine."

I hardly knew what to say, so I just offered random supportive statements. I didn't know what blood cancer was so, after I hung up, I phoned my sister, who is a retired laboratory technologist.

"I just finished talking with Mom. Do you know what's wrong with her? She says she has blood cancer. What did the doctor say? What is happening with Mom?"

"She doesn't have cancer. She's scheduled for tests at the Oshawa Hospital and has an appointment with an oncologist there."

"If it isn't cancer, why is she going to a cancer specialist?" *I'm a psychologist, not a medical professional, but I know what an oncologist is.*

"Oh," my sister said, "They see all kinds of people in oncology." *Really? I didn't think so.*

In August 2010, I'd flown east from Calgary to Ontario to see Mom and find out what was wrong. I'd picked up my rental car and driven home. As I walked up to the door, Mom came out to greet me. When I saw her, I took a little intake of breath. She had always been slim, but now she was skin and bones, her skin grey, her hair stringy. She was wearing pajamas—in the middle of the afternoon. Dad had died ten years before, so Mom was on her own now—no one to help if she fell or got sick. I hugged her as she clung to the porch railing.

I went through the door after her and we sat at our old oak kitchen table.

"I have to go to the Oshawa Hospital tomorrow. Can you take me for my appointment?"

"Yes, of course." I attempted to reassure her, "It'll be fine, I'm sure. Better to find out what's wrong. The doctors will figure out what to do." I went into the kitchen to make us sandwiches and tea for supper.

Later, I climbed the stairs to the bedroom my sister and I had shared as children, still decorated as it had been over fifty years before. The flowered wallpaper, the chenille bedspreads on the matching twin beds, the dressing table—all the same. The mice were different, though—audaciously bold since Mom had been unable to look after the house properly.

The following morning, I showered and dressed, made my mother and I tea and toast, then helped her wash and dress and find her purse. We left by the side door, with me helping her down the steps to the car.

"Have you got the information about where we're supposed to go?" I asked.

She looked at me, both eyebrows and voice raised sharply, "Of course I do! It's right here. In my purse." We drove in silence to Oshawa.

I had no idea what she was going to the hospital for—and neither did she. Mom and I sat in the waiting room for a couple of minutes until she was called into a small room set up for surgical procedures. An aide instructed her to dress in an open-back hospital gown and to get up on the gurney.

A technician came in and said, "This will hurt, but it will be over quickly," while brandishing a large hypodermic needle.

I tried to keep my anxiety to myself as I realized she was going to have a bone marrow biopsy. Mom turned to me and offered her hand to hold. Though that kind of physical intimacy was unfamiliar for the two of us, I took it. I was there to help her.

We returned two days later for the oncologist to confirm the preliminary diagnosis—multiple myeloma—stage four. The nurse scheduled multiple visits so my mother could begin a regimen of chemotherapy.

After a week of keeping my mother company, I sat in her living room and said, "Mom, you know I have to go home to Calgary tomorrow."

"I know, and I'm not looking forward to it." This was the first time I ever remembered her implying she needed me.

* * *

Once she started chemo, Mom spent her days and nights on the living room couch, too weak to climb the stairs to her bedroom. I arranged for her to have a medical alert bracelet and for a neighbour to spend at least one day a week with her. My sister organized a visiting nurse and an RPN—a registered practical nurse—to help. My brother visited every day.

Despite all this, Mom deteriorated to the point where she couldn't look after herself.

During my next visit, I sat in the living room while a social worker declared my mother unsafe to stay in her own home. I packed her clothes and prepared to take her to her new home, a nursing home in Port Hope.

Every month or so, for the five years between 2010 and 2015, I flew from Alberta to visit my mother. For those two to three week visits, I stayed alone in our old country home, and drove forty minutes back and forth to Port Hope, to sit with my Mother in the nursing home, run errands, and do her shopping—for comfortable, easy-to-remove clothing.

Due to the care Mom received in the nursing home and the chemo treatments for the multiple myeloma, she became well enough that I could take her to restaurants—her favourite outing—to Cobourg harbour to sit and watch the geese, and on drives around the countryside.

During her chemo appointments at the hospital, I sat drinking my coffee and chatting, while she endured an IV in her skinny arm, delivering the chemicals that were keeping her alive. I knew she was frightened. For two to three days after each treatment, she would be delirious and weak.

Unfortunately, unnecessary family arguments marred every visit. As we drove to The Buttermilk Café in Cobourg, Mom looked at me and said, "You know your sister is very critical of you. Maybe it's good you got away."

I sat speechless, unable to come up with a response—I didn't challenge my mother, but wondered, *why hadn't she defended me?* Protected me?

What I didn't realize or acknowledge at the time was that this would be a recurring theme for my mother and me. Why hadn't she defended me or protected me against the Teacher at Leskard school? I couldn't ask her, or confront her. It was enough for me that my mother and I were getting along, finally speaking to each other, after so many years of her hanging up the phone in fits of anger.

* * *

Visiting Leskard, the village where I grew up, and staying in our old home, when Mom was sick and living in the nursing home, disturbed me too much for a woman in her sixties—especially at night when I felt the most fear. During my earlier visits, while Mom had still been at home, I slept in my old bedroom upstairs. Then I moved to a daybed in our old dining room so I could be there to help Mom get to the toilet at night. After she went into the nursing home, I was in the house alone, with the mice and the creaking of the wind, the stairs, and flooring. I slept on the living room couch. When the sun went down, I was jittery, unable to relax, afraid to close my eyes. I locked the door and left the kitchen light on so I could see when I needed to get up in the night. In the daytime, the ghosts were safely tucked in my head, but at night they emerged to fly around the house.

My brother dropped by often with Tim Horton's coffee and my favourite crullers. He and I had always gotten along well, and still did.

I went through Mom's drawers, cleaning out mouse droppings and urine-soaked clothing, throwing out many of Mom's sweaters, socks, and scarves. I poked around the storage room upstairs—once the small bedroom belonging to me and my sister.

I knew Mom kept picture albums in the bottom drawer of the built-in cupboards in the living room. I took out wedding photos, albums from summer vacations and my parents' high school days, pictures in envelopes, and school photos.

Down in the bottom of the drawer were two framed photographs of students standing in front of Leskard School. I was in high school by the time they were taken. My sister was pictured there, as well as many children younger than me who had been in the school when I was still an elementary student. They were smiling, looking sweet, innocent, standing in neat, orderly rows according to age and height. Miss Cobbledick, the Junior teacher, stood on one side of the children, while the Teacher stood on the other side, looming over them, leering, as the children faced the photographer.

Secrets lurked around the edges, barely hinted at. I saw the images of those photographed, but not the underlying emotional turmoil, thoughts, or secrets. Those remained hidden, unacknowledged, and unhealed.

I knew from what my sister had told me, long after we were adults, that, while she was in his class, the Teacher continued to rub up against young girls. His hands had likely been on some of the girls in the picture, as they'd been when I was in the school.

I found an envelope of photographs the Teacher had taken at the Christmas concert practice in December 1962, when I was in grade eight. There were photos of the ten children who did a ballroom dance number—forever paused in the middle of a step—and three photos of Ricky Anderson, Paul Gaynor, Marilyn Gregory, and I as we acted out different scenes in the annual one-act play. Another picture was of the junior children, smiling shyly, boys in plaid shirts and corduroy trousers, girls in skirts, blouses, and cardigans, all ready to sing. One photo was of five girls who did a majorette number, short skirts revealing their legs, each of them proudly kneeling on one knee as they held their silvery, shiny batons high in the air. I would have to wait until I talked with Jill, one of my classmates, to find out the story behind this particular picture.

What if the Teacher's handprints lit up in bright colours on the skin of these girls? Or on those in the picture of the massed choir? How many would we see? Instead, the wounds remain unseen, invisible, not dealt with, and rarely spoken of.

The young girls in our village just had to endure, as I did. That's how we coped. False smiles for the camera.

When I found the photos of my sister's class, with the Teacher standing next to the children, I felt sick. He'd been there all along, in the bottom drawer of the house where I'd grown up. I took the pictures out of the drawer and threw them in the garbage—trying to magically throw him and his image out of my life.

* * *

In the spring, when I stayed in our old home while I visited Mom, I'd take a large bowl and sharp paring knife from the cutlery drawer and walk out between the apple trees to the large asparagus patch in the front garden. I'd mimic my father, stoop over, cut the stalks close to the ground, and fill the bowl so I could bring the harvest into the house. Then, my supper consisted of a pile of steamed asparagus on a plate, swimming in butter and salt.

My father was so proud of that asparagus patch. It was over fifty years old and still producing mountains of asparagus spears every spring. I've since found out that it's unusual to have an asparagus patch that produces for such a long time.

When I visited Mom at the nursing home in the winter, in order to get to our house, I slipped and slid on the hills that led up from the village—rental car companies don't supply winter tires. If I couldn't make it up the hills, I'd drive south to the seventh concession and take runs up the series of hills, each not quite as high as those on our road, the eighth concession. I remembered winters when I was young when the roads would fill with snow, and we'd have to park at the general store in the village and walk home—almost a mile—in icy weather. I didn't want to face the prospect of being stuck in a ditch alone, that far out in the country, in the cold.

After Mom went to the nursing home, there was no television reception in the house any longer—no aerial, no cable—so I watched DVDs on my computer. I shopped for groceries in Port Hope, close to Mom's nursing home, stopped at McDonald's on the 115 Highway north of Newcastle to use the internet, and rarely ate out except with Mom on our lunch outings. Periodically I stopped at a second-hand book shop in Port Hope to replenish my supply of mystery novels. Month in, month out, filling my time so I could see my mother on a regular basis. Sometimes I just sat and read in my mother's nursing home room while she slept.

Despite the chemo treatments, over the following five years, Mom grew weaker and thinner from the cancer. Finally, she couldn't move, couldn't speak, and had to be hand-fed—but she recognized me until the end. She lived until July 2015, just after her ninetieth birthday.

After the funeral and goodbyes to friends and family members, my husband and I returned home to Calgary. Over the following months, I experienced grief for my mother, though in truth, I had shed the most tears for her while I witnessed her health deteriorate. After that, emotional turmoil of another kind began to surface— memories of what had happened in the village school.

Chapter 6
My Parents - The Early Years

In addition to finding out who the villagers were back then, those who made the decision to keep the Teacher in his position despite the children's stories of molestation, my classmates, and others in the surrounding area, I knew I couldn't ignore my parents' role in what had happened.

Though I would know much more about my village and the children and adults in it by the time I finished my research, I knew most about my own family—they were my "case study" regarding what type of family lived in the village and what compelled them to make the decisions they did.

* * *

In some ways, my father was a typical man of the fifties, but one, as he said, born with a silver spoon in his mouth. His father had been a surgeon practicing in New York City, who died suddenly in 1932 when Dad was only seven. Doctor Lee was blown up in a boat off the shore of Gananoque, the small town in the Thousand Islands, Ontario, where he was born and where he and my grandmother had a summer home—a mansion, actually. When my grandfather died, my granny was in shock—her hair reportedly turned white overnight. Grampa Lee's picture was on the wall of their den during my childhood, and his memory hung like a pall over our whole family. There were rumours his death might have been related to the New York mob, but nothing was ever proven.

My Dad's mother inherited a substantial life insurance annuity in addition to their large home. My father, his brother, and my granny continued to live in their home in Gananoque until my dad and his younger brother reached their teens, and Granny had adopted a baby, my aunt, from the Catholic sisters in Kingston. At that point, Dad's Uncle Stewart insisted the family move to Oshawa where he lived, an industrial city east of Toronto, so he could supervise them. Granny, Dad, my uncle, and aunt moved to a large home in Oshawa where Granny remarried. When my father crashed his mother's car and began to smoke and drink underage, he and his brother were sent to St. Michael's private school in Toronto to tame them.

After he finished high school, Dad enrolled in Syracuse University in New York state to study forestry, but returned home before he graduated. He felt like a failure and, over the years, became angry, anxious, and depressed, and found a number of ways to deal with those feelings. One was to work hard at being a responsible bread-winner, despite having a job at General Motors he hated. Another was to control my mother and, eventually, me. Yet another was to drink.

* * *

Mom's mother had also been widowed—when my mother was fourteen years old—and my Nana turned their family home into a boarding house to make a living. Aunt Dorothea, my mother's older sister, went to secretarial school so she could get a good job and help support the family. Mom left school as soon as she could to train and then work as a stenographer in the Royal Bank in Oshawa. In addition, she was such a talented skater that she was offered a place in the Ice Capades—which she turned down. Fear of leaving all she had ever known likely played a role in this decision, but also, she wanted a nice home, a husband, and children—just like all her friends.

Mom was attracted to my dad—he was handsome, a Paul Newman lookalike, who came from a family that had much more than hers. He was a "catch" for a young woman who felt unattractive and envious of those who didn't have to scrape for every dime. When Dad dropped out of university in 1946, they were married. She got her man, but he wasn't the dream husband she wanted. Or, at least, their dreams were very different.

When I was born, my parents lived in Oshawa, Ontario, in a flat comprising the top two floors of a house owned by my father's mother, my granny, one block from Nana, my mother's mother.

In the fifties, women whose husbands had good jobs stayed home and were convinced that housework was fulfilling, suburban life was exciting, wearing the right hat, gloves, shoes, and bag would make any woman's life happy, and producing children was the highest good. I was born in 1949 and both families were thrilled to have their first grandchild.

Mom filled her life with looking after me, shopping, cooking, cleaning, visiting her mother and sister, and her bridge club. But both my mother and father's dream of having more children was thwarted after she had me. Over the years, from my mother and her sister, I heard the story of what had happened.

I must have been about two or three when my mother left me with her mother, my nana, for the morning because she had an appointment with her doctor. She wanted to see why she was not getting pregnant again as planned.

The doctor told her she'd only be able to get pregnant after some surgery. She had a tipped uterus. From her stories, I knew my mother hadn't anticipated surgery, but she and my father wanted more children.

Mom left her doctor's office. When she walked into her mother's kitchen, Nana would have immediately put the kettle on as she always did when anyone arrived. She would already have set out two cups, a bowl of sugar, and a small pitcher of milk, on the table. Mom would then have explained everything to her mother—the need for surgery and the expected outcome.

Nana had inherited fortune-telling arts from her Irish mother. The women in my family learned to respect the tea leaf patterns that meant a letter was coming, good news was on the horizon, or the splotch of leaves that might mean a baby was on its way, so I imagine she studied Mom's cup carefully, hoping to see that splotch of leaves.

The surgery was scheduled for the following month. Much later, Aunt Dorothea, my Mother's older sister, told me what had happened.

While my mother lay unaware on the operating table, expecting to awaken able to have more children, the surgeon signalled to his assistants that he was going to have a quiet word with the patient's husband, my father. He walked out into the waiting room and asked my father to accompany him to a small office to discuss what was happening in the surgery.

"We need to take the uterus out. Your wife has fibroid tumours."

The surgeon's advice as to what to do in a case like this came from a practical, no-nonsense approach, and the common belief in the fifties that a uterus taken from a young, healthy, unsuspecting woman in her mid-twenties would hurt nothing in the long run.

My father tried to take in the impact a complete hysterectomy would have on my mother and himself. He asked for a few minutes to consider things.

The surgeon was waiting. My Dad felt pressure to agree with this professional, a man who must know more than he did. He phoned my Aunt Dorothea to get her thoughts. She told me my father was crying on the phone. Confused.

She told him, "Get a second opinion. What would Norma want? This is a huge thing."

But in the end, he didn't have the courage to contradict the advice of the educated man who would permanently alter my mother's body and the future of our family.

* * *

My mother woke in the recovery room—an odd word, recovery, as she never really did recover.

Many years later, she told me what happened—how the doctor walked toward her and stood by the bedside. How he'd told her she was fine—I guess that was his belief.

My mother asked the surgeon, "Will I be able to get pregnant right away?"

He told her he'd had to remove her uterus, that he'd found fibroid tumours while he was doing the operation. Satisfied that my mother understood, he turned to go, but then told her, "You can always adopt."

It took a few minutes for my mother to realize the implication of what had been done to her while she lay unconscious on the operating table. Then she saw my father on the other side of the room and asked him if he knew she was going to wake up like this. Of course he did—he'd been partially responsible for the decision.

After a week or so, my mother was able to go home—after all, it wasn't considered major surgery.

By the time my mother told me this story, she had buried her anger and upset and the grief that must have followed. She had been violated, attacked in her sleep, left barren, and could do nothing about it. Over the years, I know she tried to accept that the operation had been necessary.

Several times she told me she hoped I wouldn't have the same condition she had and that I should have my children early if I wanted them. I didn't have any problems, though, and had my two boys in my late twenties. In addition, I know that today, my mother would likely be told that her fibroids would decrease during menopause and, unless there were significant problems, nothing needed to be done. But all this happened in the early fifties.

I don't know how much my parents discussed my father's part in the decision to remove my mother's uterus, if they ever did. Theirs was not a marriage where they talked much. Possibly he convinced her that there was no choice— or she felt it was easier to think of it that way. But things my father said over the years showed that he felt keenly the reality that he wouldn't have a male heir to carry the family name.

As I sifted through my memories of my parents, I wondered how much these events had contributed to the dissatisfaction and unhappiness in their marriage. Many years later I realized that it is not the problems couples have in their marriage, but their communication skills and willingness to talk things through that determine happiness.

At some point my parents decided to adopt. Mom wanted more children and though my father wanted more children of his own, that was not going to happen. His sister, my Aunt Bobbie, told me Dad was reluctant to adopt, but since she had been adopted by their mother and he loved her, she convinced him. Perhaps it was easier for Dad to consider adopting a daughter at that time rather than a son. I don't know. Maybe Dad thought he owed my mother this. They filled out papers and asked relatives and neighbours for references.

* * *

Mom and Dad bought their first house, a two-bedroom bungalow, in the small community of Courtice, about five miles east of Oshawa, when I was about four. We were then living on an acre of land that would have room for children to roam. Dad still had a relatively short commute to his job in General Motors and it was still easy for mom to visit Nana and her friends.

Hunting was one of Dad's favourite activities, along with fishing, so he built dog kennels for his foxhounds behind our new home. We also had a Brittany spaniel, Belle, who lived in the house with us. My father was devoted to her—a champion bird dog that could hunt pheasants and that he could show in field trials. He also wanted to breed her with other championship dogs to have more Brittany Spaniels to hunt with—and to sell. And it's possible that his love of hunting may have led to our eventual move right out into the country, but I'm getting ahead of myself.

A few months after the Catholic Children's Aid reviewed my parents' application to adopt, officials came to inspect the home that would welcome a new baby. They quickly approved the family with the man who had a regular job in the Motors, a stay-at-home mother, and a built-in big sister. Mom and Dad reassembled the brown metal crib that had been mine and set it up in my bedroom.

We made the journey to the next town, entered the Catholic Children's Aid Office, and waited for the new addition to our family. My parents gave her a new name, Bonnie.

She was a round-faced eight-month-old child, much bigger than a newborn, but I didn't know that, never having seen a new baby, or my mother pregnant. I never thought about how babies arrived in families. Our new baby was from an office where a lady walked out from behind a door and placed her in my mother's arms. She was to be my sister, to sleep beside me in my old crib while I slept in my big-girl bed.

In the 1950s, children caught a lot of diseases. My big-girl bed witnessed me coughing non-stop when I contracted whooping cough. I had red measles, and German measles (luckily my mother couldn't get pregnant by that time because, as I found out much later, German measles can cause birth deformities). But I didn't catch the mumps from my best friend Janie. My favourite stuffed animals—Bobo the brown bear, Henry the gold-coloured bear, and Penelope the blue giraffe—slept with me. When I had colds, or congestion, my mother boiled Friar's Balsam in a pot beside my bed. Unfortunately, Bobo took a nose dive into the pot, and for years after had that familiar eucalyptus-like odour!

My new sister browned easily in the sun—olive skin, my mother said—unlike my pale Irish skin, white, with freckles, like Mom's. Bonnie's hair was very dark, thick and straight as a poker—sticking out from her head—while mine was dark brown with red flecks, fine, and wavy. As she got older, she could have braids in her hair, while I could only manage pigtails—and my hair was too curly to bother with that. When we played make-believe, I would undo her braids so her hair flowed down her back like a fairy princess.

Bonnie clung to my mother, refusing to walk until nearly two years of age. She preferred that my mother carry her around on her hip. When I cuddled with my mother on the couch, she wiggled in between, pushing me from my place. She learned to be persuasive and it pleased my mother to have a child who seemed to need her so much.

My mother bonded more and more with this new child. As I was nearly five years older, I helped Mom with housework—drying the dishes, ironing and vacuuming, and eventually babysitting.

My life in Courtice was a blur of Roy Rogers and Dale Evans, orange popsicles, learning to ride a two-wheeler, and living next door to my best friend, Janie. She and I had the run of friends' gardens and her grandparents' farm just across the road. We picked pears from her grandparents' tree, and stole day-old pastries they bought and stored on their back porch.

In the summer, we hung upside down on swings and played in her playhouse. In the winter, we skated on frozen ponds edged with cattails. One day, after chewing on icicles, I leaned over the garbage bin in our kitchen and watched my first loose tooth fall out of my mouth.

Janie and I had matching green shorts and patterned blouses, black patent leather "Mary Jane" shoes, cowgirl outfits with fringed vests and skirts, and lunch pails with Roy Rogers and Dale Evans on the front. Every Saturday morning, we sat in her house or mine to watch the Cisco Kid and Poncho, Hop-along Cassidy, and the Lone Ranger.

All the children who lived on my road played together, were all invited to each other's birthday parties, and walked to school together. I remember Mrs. Greer well—our first-grade teacher in the small portable classroom on Highway 2. She was an older, empathetic woman who liked my school work so much she asked my mother if she could take my workbooks with her to a teachers' convention.

When I reached grade two, I had to prepare for my First Communion, so I walked a mile from our house to Highway 2 and waited for the bus that took me all the way to St. Gertrude's Catholic school in Oshawa. Father Mahoney, our parish priest, visited the classrooms to talk to the children. At the end of the year, I was awarded the prize for highest marks in the class—a glow-in-the-dark Jesus on a pink cross that terrified me. But I was safe there, the same as all the other children, preparing for life as a proper Catholic girl.

The summer I was eight and a half and my sister turned three, I waved goodbye to Janie, and my family drove from that suburban community east of Oshawa to our new home just west of Leskard, a village way, way out in the country.

We might have been all right as a family had we not moved to the country, though it's impossible to say. We did move and our lives changed forever. We were faced with challenges my parents couldn't have foreseen and didn't deal with effectively. Perhaps their problem was as simple as bad communication, or lack of courage, but I suspect the issues were much deeper than that.

Chapter 7
We Move To Leskard

Leskard is one of many old villages, some bigger, some smaller, scattered around Clarke Township, twenty miles east of Oshawa, fifty miles east of Toronto. Nearest to us was Kirby, just to the southeast. Tyrone was to the west, Kendal, a bigger village, further to the east, and Orono, a much bigger village, to the south of us. Orono seemed to me like a real town. It was an old established village with many lovely century homes. There was a main street with a Stedman's five to a dollar store, a CIBC bank, a service station, a drug store, a café with pool hall, two grocery stores, an apartment building that had been a hotel, a post office, a doctor's office, a town hall, a weekly newspaper—*The Orono Times*—a United church, an elementary school and high school combined, and a funeral home. There was a large cemetery, and a harness racing track on grounds used for the Fall fair. Orono also had an arena for skating, hockey, and the fair displays, and a large park with an outdoor swimming pool.

Suddenly we were newcomers in a rural area filled mainly with farm families, many of whose ancestors had been there for over a hundred years. My family had stepped into a rural culture they were unfamiliar with and that had existed long before we came. Though only a half hour drive east from Oshawa, the town where my parents had grown up, it might as well have been the other side of the moon. My life completely changed—though how much, I could never have predicted at the time.

***

My assumption is that the move to the country was all Dad's idea. I know in retrospect that my father had dreams, but exactly what he was searching for in his quest for land and country living, I didn't and couldn't know at the time. Perhaps he looked upon our new home as a type of rural paradise. However, even today, I have no idea why my parents looked to this particular area for our new home—where we knew no one.

Dad had studied forestry at Syracuse University in New York State, but my mother said he dropped out due to "nervous problems." He worked in the Ontario Forestry department in Toronto for a while but quit because of the long commute from Oshawa. After that, he reluctantly took a job on the line at General Motors, despite loving wide-open fields, forests, animals, and birds.

My parents had applied for a Veterans Land Act loan to buy the Davy Farm, a four-hundred-acre farm established in 1840, but were turned down. Neither he nor my mother had any farming experience. Instead, the VLA loaned them enough to buy part of the Davy farm—our "new" house, with a drive shed, a barn and ten acres of land. Not enough to farm. Dad still had to make the twenty-mile commute to Oshawa to his job at General Motors.

In our new home, we were living on a hill, next to endless fields at the edge of a huge valley where the village of Leskard sat. From our house, we could only see the barn on the next farm, about a quarter of a mile away, but if we looked south, we could see all the way to Lake Ontario. After my mother held her first bridge party in our country home, her friends refused to return—said it was too far for them to drive from Oshawa.

* * *

During that first summer in our new home, we tried to find our way as country dwellers. Dad looked out one day and saw a boy on a tractor, out in our field, ploughing. He ran out to talk with him and then came back to the house to tell Mom what had happened. I remember that conversation.

"That boy says his family always ploughs and plants that field—corn some years, hay others. He said he could do it—without even telling us!"

"What did you say to him?" Mom asked.

"I told him I would talk with his father about this, but, for now, he had to stop. He left, but he sure wasn't happy. He told me he had 'the right' to plough our field. I'm going down the road to see his father."

When Dad came back from seeing Mr. Bayley, he was furious. "Bayley says he had an agreement with the Davys that he could use that field. Now he wants me to pay his son for ploughing part of the field, when I didn't even ask him!" If Dad had expected a welcome to the country, he was mistaken.

When school started in September, the youngest Bayley boy came up to me at recess, "Your Dad was wrong to stop my family from ploughing the field." *I was eight years old, what could I do about any of that?* According to Timmy, we were just newcomers. Mr. and Mrs. Bayley were never all that friendly toward our family all the time we lived there, but their children were.

* * *

We were on a steep learning curve to understand the ways of the village families and the farmers in the area—their connections, their relationships, and informal agreements—all things I know my father hadn't anticipated. He naively thought that living in the country would be similar to living in the suburb we had just left—except it would be in the wide outdoors. He was wrong. In addition to learning "country ways," we also had to deal with weather, our old house, and the physical difficulties of living out in the wilds.

Our new-old home had many beautiful decorative features, but it creaked and screeched in the hilltop winds as though a tornado was always blowing. On the main floor, the living room and dining room were large with polished pine floors and ceilings well over eight feet in height. I knew this because it was a point of pride for my Dad, "Eight-and-a-half foot ceilings! You don't get those anymore!"

In some ways, when we moved to the country, we'd moved back in time. In our suburban home in Courtice, we used a normal 1950s black rotary phone. Now we used a hand-cranked, polished-wood-cased phone that was mounted on the wall, with a Bakelite ear piece that hung on the left side and a metal mouthpiece that stuck out at a steep angle from the middle of the large box. There were nearly twenty people on the party line, so any time I wanted to use the phone, I had to pick up the earpiece and listen. If there was no one talking on the line, I could call a neighbour if I knew their home ring, or the operator to connect to anyone outside the area. Mom warned me, "Never say anything personal on the phone! You can never tell if someone might be listening in."

My sister and I shared a small bedroom with no windows and plaster walls that gave way if you pushed the wallpaper very hard. I was frightened of whatever lay underneath the pink and yellow roses printed on the surface of the wallpaper. I ripped holes in the roses and dug shallow pits into the plaster underneath. Searching for demons? Trying to let them out?

Each night, I'd lie in bed, looking away from the wall beside my bed toward my sister, and terrify myself with the thought that something might attack me. After I had built up enough courage to turn back toward the wall, the roses were undisturbed. No matter how many times I did this, I felt afraid. Even the pictures of Ricky Nelson, clipped from the backs of comic books and pasted onto the wall at the end of my bed, couldn't protect me.

In winter, if we woke up huddling and shivering under our blankets, we knew that the fire in the furnace had died. One morning the temperature dropped to the freezing point. Dad hadn't gone down to the basement in the middle of the night to shovel in coal. However, if the electricity went out, which happened quite often, the coal furnace could keep on pouring out heat. My mother, sister, and I would play board games by the light of oil lamps or candles, while staring out at the blackness outside our windows. Ice storms regularly took down the electrical wires, so we always had the lamps and candles ready.

We had a chemical toilet in the upstairs room next to our bedroom, instead of a modern toilet in the bathroom. Basically, it was a three-foot high metal bucket with a toilet seat on top—an indoor "outhouse." Dumping it was Dad's job.

On dumping day, we knew the routine. He put on his special leather "toilet dumping gloves" in preparation. Dad's staccato speech and the grim set of his mouth let us know he was girding himself for battle.

He barked orders at all of us. "Norma, I want you and the kids to stay out of the way. Get out of the hallway, the living room, and the dining room so I can come through."

He had to lift the bucket—stinking, heavy, full of the family's excrement—carry it downstairs, yelling at everyone as he went, walk through the house, out the door, and over to the field. We kids weren't allowed anywhere near the field either. He emptied the bucket into a hole he'd dug, shovelled it over, then carried the bucket back upstairs and replaced the toilet seat.

I learned much later that other people in the village had these "toilets" too, but no one ever talked about it.

When we first moved in, indoor plumbing in our country house was restricted to the kitchen taps and a large sink in a room on the main floor that would eventually become our bathroom. Each morning before school, I went downstairs to the large sink, filled it full of soapy water and washed myself with a facecloth—no tub or shower to use. It seemed to take hours, but then I did dawdle.

"Karen, hurry up and get dressed. Your cereal will be cold and you'll be late for school." Every morning, same routine. Perhaps I was in no hurry to get to school.

By the time I was about ten or eleven, we'd had a bathroom installed in our home, with a small sink, tub, and normal flush toilet. But to conserve water, there were rules. We were warned not to use much water if we bathed in the tub—about four inches maximum—and not to flush the toilet using the flush handle. We had a bucket beside the toilet that we had to fill with water to pour down the toilet when we needed to. I did this conscientiously, as I didn't want anyone in the family to see anything that came out of my body I considered embarrassing—but others in the family didn't seem to do this.

I was often nervous to enter the bathroom and lift the toilet lid—I could be greeted by a filled toilet bowl. Then I would use the bucket filled with water to flush away someone else's waste. Only then did I feel able to use the toilet myself. I couldn't complain because I would have to put into words what I was seeing in the toilet and what I was doing to eliminate the problem. And we never discussed anything like that in my family.

Today, the irony doesn't escape me that, though it was private and personal, it was there for all of us to see. And that it was up to me to get rid of someone else's shit.

* * *

When I went down into the cellar, I opened a small door in the kitchen, bent down so I wouldn't hit my head on the angled ceiling, and turned my feet slightly sideways so they would fit on the narrow stairs, smoothed by over one hundred years of use. My sister was terrified of the cellar—dark and clammy with field-stone walls and a dirt floor. The octopus furnace that had to be shovel-fed with coal dominated the left side of the basement. To the right of the stairs sat a six-foot-high cement cistern where water collected during rain storms—our wash water supply—not for drinking due to the dead mice, moles, and occasional squirrel that floated on top of the water. Sometimes Dad went down to the cellar, climbed the ladder at the side of the cistern, checked the water to see how clear it looked, and dumped in some liquid bleach.

If it hadn't rained in a while and the water level in the cistern was low, he called the local water delivery man. Before driving up the hill to our house, Mr. Pethick stopped in the village to fill up his tank truck with water from the creek. He'd pull into our yard and stick a hose long enough to reach from the truck and through the cellar window, so he could pump water into the cistern. But he delivered more than water. He was full of local gossip that kept Dad entertained while they waited for the cistern to fill—a guilty pleasure for my father who said he didn't approve of tittle tattle.

Chapter 8
School And Life In The Village

In September 1957, leaving Belle barking and jumping, wanting to come along, I walked down our laneway and the country road, through the village and up to the two-storey white clapboard village school. There were two doors on the front of the building, one for boys and one for girls. I opened the door on the right, went into the girls' cloakroom area, and knocked on the classroom door. My new Teacher opened it and ushered me in.

Leskard school, built in 1860, was nothing like the Catholic school I'd attended in Oshawa where each grade had its own classroom. There were only two classrooms in total. Upstairs was the junior room, grades one to three. The downstairs room held Grades four to eight. I should have been starting grade three, but, after a couple of weeks, was accelerated into grade four, so stayed downstairs with the "big kids."

The Teacher always wore a dark blue suit and white shirt. He must have bought shirts that were too small—the collar squeezed his neck until his bald head stood like a pumpkin on a stand—a stand made of stiff cloth. He seemed old to me, though I realize now he was only twenty-seven. Back then he seemed ancient.

His fat white fingers stuck out of the sleeves of his suit, and when he directed us in singing, they punched the air and pointed as though they could force the songs out of us. The face the Teacher presented to the village was of a competent teacher, yet when I asked him to show me where the Amazon River was, he looked for it on a map of Africa.

The Teacher played with the students at recess, laughing as he chased the girls, trying to join our games. I didn't remember any teacher doing that before. When he saw us with our double-dutch skipping ropes, he came over and took one end to turn. I didn't want to jump into the turning ropes and have my skirt go flying up in front of him, but it was that or forget about skipping at recess.

* * *

Jill Bayley became a close friend as soon as I started school. She and I were in the same grade, along with Ricky Anderson and Janie Gregory, so the four of us sat in the same row. Jill was the same age as me but a head shorter. She was a quiet girl, friendly, not silly or rambunctious, so the two of us got along well.

She wore dresses that hung on her. She never had a chance to grow into them, because each school year brought new dresses that floated around her tiny body like parachute silk.

"Mom, Jill's dresses always hang way past her knees."

My Mother replied, "I think her mother matches her dress size to her age when she orders from the Eaton's catalogue, rather than buying something that will fit."

"But her brothers' clothes fit them."

"Well, likely the boys are all average height and weight for their ages. Jill is very small, so, at age ten, size ten is much too big.

On a hot summer afternoon, I walked down the dirt road to Jill's farm to ask if she would explore with me. As I walked into her yard, I heard one of her family dogs snarling and yapping as it rushed up to me. He leaped up on my leg and sank his teeth into my knee before I could get out of the way. I screamed, began to cry, and looked to see blood dripping down my leg.

"The dogs are here to protect the house. What did you expect?" Did Jill's father blame me for causing the dog to bite?

Her mother came out of the house and gave me a cloth to stop the bleeding. Then Jill's oldest brother Kevin came out of the house with a large band-aid. I wiped my leg, put the band-aid on the tooth marks. and left with Jill. We walked across open fields, climbing over fences to avoid the cows—especially the bull. We picked apples off the trees, making sure to rub them on our shirts before we ate them.

When I got home hours later, my mother took one look at my leg, heard the story of the Bayley's dog biting me, and called to my father, "Look at Karen's leg. We're going to the doctor's office."

Rabies was rampant at that time in Southern Ontario, and my Dad often warned us against animals acting strangely—foxes or coyotes that might approach when normally they would run away. My parents bundled me into the car and drove to Orono.

The doctor examined my leg and said to my parents, "That farm dog was just protecting its property—that's not an irrational act, so it's unlikely that it's rabies. I'll give your daughter a tetanus shot."

And we went home. But Mom and Dad were angry. Jill's parents hadn't even bothered to phone to tell them what had happened.

* * *

When we drove east from our house, we descended the hills to get to the main corner of the village where the general store stood. Dad collected books about the history of the area and told me that Leskard was an old village, originally much larger, with wood and grain mills, several stores, a hotel, and a couple of churches. It was initially settled by Irish protestants, followed by settlers from England who spread out over several concessions in the area. The land was mainly farmed. Scottish and Irish stonemasons had built many of the local stone houses.

The 1851 Clarke Township census showed a population of 6,190, with only 205 Catholics, but, despite the very few Catholics in the township, twelve Orange lodges formed after Protestant Irish had populated the area—they brought their prejudices with them. To them, Catholics were lazy, wild, had too many children, were too verbose and followed the Pope. Settlement by Irish Catholics was mainly due to the Great starvation of the 1840s and fifties. Even in 1900, there was only one Catholic church and it was in Newcastle, a small town in the south part of the township.

One Saturday in July, my father came home spewing and spitting that he'd been held up in the nearby town of Bowmanville by the Orangemen's parade held to celebrate the Glorious Twelfth (of July). His anger was perhaps understandable, as the Orange Lodge, strong in this largely protestant area, still wanted to rid the world of Irish Catholics.

When I'd transferred from a large suburban Catholic school where I'd been the same as all the other children, protected by all the angels and saints in the Catholic church, to the village public school, I was the only Catholic child—

and no longer protected. My mother wrote a note to my new Teacher saying that, since the Catholic Lord's Prayer ended a couple of sentences short of the Protestant prayer, could I stop reciting at the end of the Catholic version? We Catholics had strict rules we had to obey and an overwhelming sense of guilt if we didn't. I handed the note to the Teacher.

When the Teacher said, "Just stop where you're used to," I breathed a sigh of relief.

When I was skipping rope during a school recess period and asked one boy to move out of the way, he yelled, "That's just like a Catholic for you!" revealing the long-held prejudice that remained among some farm folks in the area. I wondered if he'd heard this sort of thing at home.

I was different in other ways, too. I was "new." I wasn't related to anyone in the village. I was interested in school work, reading, and learning. I was accused by farm boys of using "big words." Perhaps my classmates knew they would eventually work on their family farm, at Curve Ply in Orono, the Newcastle box factory, or in the General Motors plant twenty miles away, so they wouldn't need higher education? I didn't know. Dad came from an educated family that had sent him to a private Catholic school. He sorely regretted not staying in university. He worked at GM as a foreman, but both my parents were avid readers and wanted their children to go to university.

* * *

My mother was hesitant about the village, but she suggested that if our family was to be accepted, we had to participate in events held in the village. At dinner one night, she said, "I talked to Father Malane last Sunday to get permission for us to help with the village Strawberry Social."

It was held at the end of June every year in the hall attached to the back of the village church.

"Then I talked to Mrs. Chater in the village. She was surprised we were going to volunteer, but also really pleased, very welcoming."

I was excited. I loved social events. "What do we have to do? What can I wear?"

Mom said she'd make me a dress. She had a length of yellow gingham and green rick rack to trim the sleeves. I wore the new dress with an apron over it as Mom and I served heaping plates of meat and vegetables, followed by strawberry pie and whipped cream, to people who'd come from miles around. Long tables covered with white tablecloths were crammed with those who'd paid seventy-five cents for the supper, profits to go to the church. I loved finally feeling part of the village.

However, my mother was confusing. Though she made that effort, she didn't really want to be a villager. She conceded that I had to go to the village school, we had to pick up our mail and do some grocery shopping at the general store, but she didn't want to "mix." She saw people standing around in the store gossiping and didn't approve.

I tried to figure out my mother's attitude. When we lived in Courtice, I was allowed to play with the children on Courtice Road, walk to the store with friends, and be gone the whole day with Janie and other playmates. Here in the country, everything changed. She was reluctant for me to play with local children on Saturdays, completely isolating me—while Dad encouraged me.

What was my mother so fearful of? Did village children do terrible things? Unforgivable things? Maybe it was "catchy"—something physical that would reach out and grab me. Mom's judgement and her uncertainty constantly swirled around me. I worried that there was something that would infect my mind and change who I was. Something I had to resist. More importantly, if the village was cursed, why had we moved here? But perhaps my mother intuitively knew more than she realized.

Chapter 9
Home Issues

When I began this journey to explore what had happened in my village school, why the people in the village had allowed their children to go to a school where a pedophile was teaching, I knew I would have to describe my parents. I would have to delve into their issues, their relationship, and their decision to allow us, their two daughters, to go to that school. As I did this, I now saw it all with adult eyes.

Yes, I did have to face the village that my mother only reluctantly wanted to acknowledge, but I also faced problems at home.

Each evening my family would sit around the antique oak table for dinner. Mom lit a candle in the middle of the table and then we said grace. It was a ritual I relied on. But our family didn't talk during dinner, at least not about anything important, chatty or controversial. We followed an unwritten rule that said no one could laugh, cry, or relax. We rarely invited anyone to dinner. We would eat quietly, get up, and do the dishes.

I listened silently while I heard my mother's gossip and complaints as she washed and I dried.

"Mrs. Anderson's parents are first cousins—that's why she's so crazy."

I went to school with the Anderson children.

"Girls who get into cars with boys are asking for it."

Asking for what? Something must happen in cars that didn't happen anywhere else.

"June Higgins in the village *had* to get married—and she's only seventeen!"

At such a young age, I didn't understand how pregnancy worked, nor that I was learning my mother's greatest fear.

I heard repeatedly that the dentist I went to had asked my mother to marry him when they were young — "He and his wife have a big house in Oshawa."

She pointed this house out to me whenever we went to Oshawa to shop. Was she sorry she lived with us? Was she not happy with Dad?

"I read in a magazine that women who like purple are bad."

The house across from the school was painted purple.

She stressed to me that her favourite colour was yellow. This she told me in an almost reverential tone, as though I had to agree that it was, indeed, the most beautiful colour ever. There could be no other colour as wonderful because she had declared it the best. My mother's choices, her opinions, were what mattered. I didn't mention that my favourite colour was red. I wasn't sure what her reaction would be. It was just easier to agree with her.

When my sister was old enough to help with the dishes, we argued about who got to wash, who would have to dry. Washing the dishes was more fun than drying—I would show my sister how to trap air in a glass and lower it into the water, bubbles releasing as I turned the glass to one side. Drying was boring. When she was older she could wash, but making the process fun was more important than time to us, and my mother would yell that it was taking us too long to finish this particular chore.

"Cinderella, Cinderella, all I hear is Cinderella." Mom often sang this Disney movie theme song when we all did the dishes together. Maybe it summed up her belief that she was forever left at home while other women, more attractive or more privileged than her, went to the ball. Though I sensed it, I didn't know how isolated and lonely my mother was, forgotten in the country, her friends and family miles away.

* * *

My father was not Prince Charming, despite coming from a wealthy and educated family and growing up in a huge home. His devotion to my mother and our family was real, but he never brought a glass slipper to transform her life— just demands to make the foods he liked and to keep the children quiet. Dad was hard-working and dedicated to providing for his family, but he was a loner who preferred hunting, fishing, and walking in the bush to being at home.

Mrs. Grey, a woman who lived about a quarter of a mile away, brought over a pie one day and a cake another. Mom had a new friend, one that lived next door, in rural terms. I knew her sons, Ben and Daniel. Ben was in the village school, a grade ahead of me. Daniel was in high school— maybe fifteen or sixteen years old.

In the summer, a year after we moved in, Daniel started coming over to visit. I liked having someone—anyone—drop over. He would draw pictures with me even though I was so much younger. We'd stick them up on the playroom wall. But the more he visited, the more uncomfortable I became. He and my mother laughed together too much. I heard her excitement, the tone of her voice like melting caramels.

One day he never came back. I heard my father tell Mom he'd told Daniel's father not to let his son come over any more. Problem solved. Well, my discomfort problem anyway. Perhaps not everything was solved for my mother.

* * *

Sometime in the summer of 1958, the summer after we moved to Leskard, when I was nine and a half, my parents, my sister and I drove to the Catholic Children's Aid office in Port Hope to adopt a new baby—a boy this time. I loved my brother from the moment we got him. He and I seemed to have a special bond, which remains to this day. I babysat him, changed him, played with him, and when he was older, I would stop in his room as I made my way to bed, so he and I could talk.

* * *

When I was about eleven, my mother made an appointment with her doctor to talk about how unhappy she was. I heard the whole story while we did the dishes.

She'd explained to the doctor how she was feeling, and his first question to her was, "What things do you do for yourself?"

She looked at me, a plate in her hand, and said, "I didn't understand what he was talking about, but then he asked me, 'Do you do anything outside the home? Hobbies, friends, clubs?'" Mom told him, "No. Nothing."

I wondered if she told him how often she got angry? Screamed at my sister and I for no reason? That she had yelled at me, "You're too old to play with silly paper dolls. You should do something intelligent." Did she tell the doctor that she ran after me with a glass of water and poured it over my head as I cowered on the floor?

Did she tell him about the time she said to me, "You listen to CHUM radio too much! That pop music is terrible." She then went into the living room, pulled out a huge music album with 78 rpm records, took one out, and put it on the record player. "Here, listen to something decent. Gershwin instead of the top ten."

As it turned out, I loved Gershwin—so much that I played *Rhapsody in Blue* and the piano concertos over and over. Too often for Mom.

"Do you have to keep playing that? Play something else."

Mom often confused me.

She repeatedly told me about her conversation with her doctor. "He told me, 'I can give you something that will relax you, but I also want you to find some activity for yourself.' He gave me a prescription for phenobarbital."

That didn't mean much to me at the time, but many years later I learned that phenobarbital was known as one of the "Mother's Little Helpers," made famous by the Stones' song of the same name. Many barbiturates were introduced in the sixties but this strong, addictive drug was *my* mother's "little helper." I remember Mom excitedly telling me she had to take her "phenobarbs" at certain times of the day. My mother's doctor was likely wiser than most, though, because he advised her to find a hobby or something she wanted to do for herself—not just take the drug.

Mom had worked at the Royal Bank in Oshawa when she was single. She wanted to work when her children were all in school. The woman who ran Hamilton's insurance in Orono needed a bookkeeper, and Mom desperately wanted that job.

Dad's response? "No wife of mine is going to work."

At twelve, I was old enough to babysit my younger sister and brother, so Mom, along with Mrs. Grant from the village, joined an art group that met once a week in the instructor's home in Orono, about five miles away. This became my mother's first lifeline. Then she started swim lessons—about twenty miles away in Oshawa. After she earned her gold medallion, she graduated to synchronized swimming, which became her real love. In her last years, when she was in the nursing home, she told me, "Synchro saved my life."

At that time, nothing else changed in our family, but my mother had her medication and her lessons. Dad had succeeded in preventing Mom from working, but the doctor said she must do some activities and my father couldn't argue with the doctor. He still grumbled, though, particularly when she went out on the nights he was home in the evenings after working the day shift at the motors.

After a particularly loud session of grumbling, Mom got into the car and drove down the dark country road. She told me she stopped the car at the side of the road and laid her head on the steering wheel, crying, thinking perhaps she should go home as Dad wanted. But something rose up in her chest—a feeling of defiance. She wiped her face, turned the key in the ignition, and drove the rest of the way to her swim lessons. Of course, I learned all this when Mom and I had our after-dinner dishwashing sessions. In lieu of friends her own age, I had become my mother's confidante.

Chapter 10
My Family Is A Case Study

Every Saturday, Dad started drinking beer shortly before noon. If we were lucky, he wouldn't be passed out by suppertime. One Saturday, when Dad had only had two or three beers, he moved around the kitchen looking for a large pot to make New England boiled dinner. It didn't sound all that appealing to me, but someone at work had told him about this dish, and Dad thought it sounded amazing. Of course, he engaged Mom in the preparations—peeling and chopping the potatoes and carrots, onions and cabbage. He prepared the meat—corned beef he'd had my mother buy at the supermarket.

Dad was fun when he'd only had a couple—more fun than Mom as she stood in the kitchen with a stony look on her face doing his bidding. He came out into the living room and put on some music—Julie London, his favourite singer—then reached out his arms toward me. "Come on. Dance with your old dad." He twirled me around the floor for a minute or two and then went back into the kitchen to supervise my mother.

"Do you know," he said, loudly enough for me to hear, "what the difference is between your mother and Julie London? After all, they're both women."

I responded with my well-rehearsed reply, "Yes, but with Julie London, it's easier to tell."

I was happy to be Dad's co-conspirator. I never thought to look at my mother's face as Dad and I laughed as though this insult was the most hilarious thing in the world. At age ten or eleven, I never even realized it *was* an insult. And my mother said nothing.

Most weekends, though, Dad passed out long before supper time. Mom, my sister, brother, and I would eat our supper and then watch television. If the television was too loud in the living room, right under the master bedroom, we'd hear a loud "BANG, BANG, BANG" from the floor above—my father signalling that he could hear the television. Mom dutifully turned down the volume every time. I waited for that thumping and my heart would pound with guilt every time I heard it. It was as if a blanket of oppression covered us no matter what we did.

* * *

When I was about twelve, my sister and I moved down the upstairs hall of our house into a room as large as our parents' master bedroom. Mom consulted decorating magazines so she could decide on wallpaper, linoleum, bed spreads, window coverings, and the colour to paint my desk. At a local auction sale, Mom and Dad bought a dressing table with a large oval mirror that sat in the corner of our room.

We finally had a bedroom window! It faced east toward the village and, when I sat at my robin-egg-blue desk, I could see the hills on the other side of the deep valley and the tree tops below the hills. Nothing of the village.

My mother longed to have a beautiful home. When we drove into town for shopping, she pointed out houses she liked. "That one is grey and so simple," she'd say. "I'd love to live there." Or, motioning towards a large house on a hill in Oshawa, forgetting how many times she'd repeated it, said, "The man who lives there is a dentist. He asked me to marry him when we were in high school."

She knew there was a corner fireplace in our country living room, covered up by wallboard, and often talked about how rare it was to find a corner fireplace in a century farmhouse. She showed me a picture of one in her historic home magazine and said ours must look just the same. But I only ever saw it in the photograph.

* * *

One night at dinner, as my sister, mother, father, and I were seated around the table, quietly eating, I suddenly realized that I was looking down at the dining table—from the ceiling. I know this will sound impossible to many people, but I could see the whole family—even myself. I barely had time to register what had happened when fear took over and propelled me back into my body. No one seemed to realize I'd "left" for a few seconds, so I just continued to eat. I cleared the table after everyone had finished the meal, and tried to make sense of what had happened. As my sister and I did the dishes, I realized I had escaped—only for a few seconds—but I had escaped. It was not until I was a psychologist that I realized I had disassociated—felt separate from my surroundings—likely due to stress.

Chapter 11
I Begin My Interviews - My Classmate, Jill

When Jill Bayley and I spoke again as adults, I noticed she was still very petite and slim, now dressed suitably in clothes that fit her. My Mother had told me some years before that she had run into Jill in Bowmanville one day and was both surprised and impressed at how nice Jill looked, how well-dressed. A contrast to how she had looked when we were in Leskard school.

I spoke with her first at the lunch in the village church, and later at the Bowmanville Family Restaurant, a Bowmanville institution of family cooking. We talked about what had happened to her from the time I'd known her as a child.

Jill's first husband left her for her best friend and she had to raise her son on her own—with very little money. So, she went back to school, trained as a home care nurse, and remarried. She said she was fine now, with the support her new husband and her faith gave her.

Then she told me about her early home life.

When she got home from school, no matter how sunny the day, she came into a house that, for her, contained no happy memories. The large oval dining table, where all the family sat for meals, was piled in the centre with dishes, glassware, cups, and cereal boxes from the last meal.

Jill would skirt the table, pick up the dishes, spoons, knives, and forks from breakfast, and scrape the leftovers into the slops bucket. Later, she might take that out to the barn for the animals, but first she piled the dishes into the wash pan in the pantry sink, and filled it with hot soapy water. While the dishes soaked, she'd take the broom and sweep the floor.

She was at the beck and call of her brothers. *Boys are for doing the work. Girls don't matter.* Jill had heard this so many times from her father that she automatically repeated it to herself—and her mother went along with it.

She peeled potatoes—enough for seven, including herself, her mother Mary, father Sid, and her four brothers. She filled a huge pot with water, put in the potatoes, and carried the pot to the stove so the potatoes would be cooking when her mother came home from work, teaching in a one-room school in the hills north of the village. Lastly, Jill washed and dried the dishes, returning most of them to the edge of the table in preparation for supper.

Her mother would be home soon to put on vegetables from the garden, and to warm up the rest of the roast left from Sunday. *When her mother got home, she would tell her. This time she would tell her.*

* * *

Jill sat down last at the dinner table—after the dishes of potatoes, meat slices, and vegetables had circled around and the spoons and forks of her father and brothers had almost emptied the bowls. After the bread basket, once stacked high with slices of white bread, had nearly been stripped, she pushed the few bits of potato left in the bowl onto her plate, along with scraps of meat and the crust of bread left in the bottom of the bread basket. She took the crust and rubbed it into the meat bowl to soak up the juice sitting at the bottom.

Finally, near the end of the meal, Jill's mother carried an apple pie out of the pantry, cut into five large pieces. The boys and Jill's father each scooped a slice onto their dinner plates. Jill looked at her mother who told her the slices would be too small if she cut ones for the two of them. Besides, the boys were the ones who did the farm work.

Her mother made a large pot of tea and carried it and five cups into the living room. She came back into the kitchen to get the milk, sugar, and spoons, and returned to the living room. One of Jill's brothers turned on the television. Mary poured the tea and passed around the cups, a jug of milk and the pot of sugar.

Then she returned to the dining table, sat down, and reached into her briefcase to get out her students' work for marking. Jill sat at the other end of the table and took out her math textbook and workbook so she could do her homework.

Jill wondered, should she bother her mother? She told me that she wanted her mother to know what had happened at school, so she said, "Mama, do you remember a week or so ago when I was late from school and didn't get the potatoes on in time? Dinner was a bit late that night?"

"Yes, you were late doing your chores." Jill's mother was only half-listening as she reached down into her bag to find her red pencil.

"I was kept late at school by the Teacher."

Distractedly, "Why? What did you do?" She found the pencil and faced the pile of workbooks in front of her.

"I didn't do anything. He said I had to stay late so he could help me with my arithmetic."

"Didn't you do your work?" Now she was looking at Jill across the table.

"I did most of it."

"Well, that's what happens if you don't finish your work."

Her mother was irritated, and just wanted to get on with her marking, but Jill continued to explain anyway. "I couldn't do it all that time. I tried to tell him, but he told me to stay in when all the rest of the kids left."

"So, you didn't do all your work and he kept you in."

"He locked the door."

By this time, Jill's mother's voice was raised, "What then?"

"He crouched down beside my desk, and then he put his hand up my leg under my dress."

Jill explained to me that, though she had wanted her mother to know, she soon realized the conversation was not going well. Her mother half-rose from her chair and yelled, "Oh, not you too." Apparently, her mother had had two girls in her school that came to her with similar stories, but she assumed they lied and thought too much about sex.

As Jill sat there feeling worse and worse, her mother continued, her voice filled with anger, "Children lie. Little girls lie. I know they do. But I never thought you would. I taught Mr. Pollard when he was young. Little Jimmie was a sweet boy. Don't you say one word against him! He and his parents are family, and they're a good family—respected, one of the oldest families in the county."

Silently Jill mouthed, "But I'm not lying."

Her mother had continued, "I don't want to hear another word about this—and don't even think about saying anything about your teacher in the village." Then she gestured with her hand. "Go, just go. I don't want to see you or talk about this again."

Jill got up from the table, gathered her books, walked to the top of the cellar steps, and sat down to finish her homework.

Later, when everyone headed up the stairs to their rooms for the night, Jill looked around to find a place to sleep—usually the couch in the living room or the stuffed chair in the corner of the dining room. She had no room of her own. She knew she just had to look after herself and keep quiet.

* * *

When we were children, I had no idea that the Teacher had molested her, that her mother didn't believe her, and that she had no bedroom of her own. It amazed me how little I knew then about what happened in my classmates' families— even someone who was a friend. But others in the village must have realized that Jill didn't have anyone to give her support—she would stop in at Cathy Spry's house in the morning so Cathy's mother could help her with her hair before school.

We children never shared with each other that some families had left their daughters to fend for themselves with a child molester—including my own, and those of the two women who had said "me, too" at the church gathering.

* * *

I continued sitting and talking with Jill at the Bowmanville Family Restaurant, discussing horrors over salads and sandwiches.

She asked if I had ever noticed boys trying to get close to the school windows, laughing and fighting to get on top of one another's shoulders? I hadn't.

Jill said, "Didn't you ever see that the Teacher locks the school door at recess and lunch hour? The boys want to see what he's doing. I don't think they could see anything though."

Chapter 12
The Bullies

Because the Teacher locked himself inside the school when he molested the girls, he wasn't supervising what went on outside.

Three of the older boys were bullies and several of the younger ones looked as though they were in training with them. When there was no one to stop them, they teased the children they felt were vulnerable - calling names, ridiculing, slapping and punching.

One June morning, the Teacher announced recess and I went outside with all the rest of the children. I looked over towards the maple trees at the side of the baseball diamond where the big boys, the bullies, were already lining up to do their worst to us, the younger kids. *Oh, no,* went through my head as I heard the familiar taunts about my last name, Lee - "Chinese," "lee-flea." There was not much originality, but their insults were fear-inducing when combined with pushes and punches.

That recess, the Teacher came out to organize a game of Red Rover we all had to participate in. I hated this game. He divided all the students up into two teams, roughly even in their make-up of small to large children. Everyone had to hold hands, the two teams facing each other. When a child called out the name of someone on the opposing team, "Red Rover, Red Rover, let Debbie come over," that child would run as fast as possible to break through the hands of two children on the other team. If you couldn't break through, you belonged to the opposing team. The side with the most children at the end was the winner.

Of course, when called over, you would try to break through the arms of the smallest children first - either you broke through or at least if you couldn't, it wasn't dangerous. But as the smaller children were eliminated, you had no choice but to try to break through the arms of the much larger boys. There was no way you could do it. When the bigger boys were called over, they would also try to go through the smallest children. They would run as fast as they could and ram into their arms. Sometimes it felt as though my arm would break - and the Teacher stood by and did nothing to intervene.

* * *

Dodging big boys at recess, trying to avoid being cornered by them, teased and hit by them - that was just life. One of the big boys pushed Philip Loucks so hard he fell face first and broke his front tooth on the cement porch of the school, but that was just boys being boys - not real violence. He couldn't afford to get his tooth repaired until he left home to work.

Another boy stood out for me. Dan - Al's younger brother. He was quiet, kind, slight for his age and wore his hair slicked back in a ducktail like Ricky Nelson. He never teased me. He was determined and loved hockey, which he played from age twelve. The nearest arena was in Orono, and with no one willing to pick him up, Dan walked home many nights. Five miles. In the dark. With his loaded hockey bag over his shoulder. Some nights, other townsfolk let him stay at their place so he didn't have to walk. Some people helped others, but no one spoke about it. That was just the way it was.

Dan did well for himself, married young to a wonderful woman, had children, and rose to a responsible position in his job in the motors. He is quiet and kind to this day.

* * *

In late Fall, at the beginning of the cold weather, the Teacher sent the older boys outside during class time to dam the creek at the bottom of the hill in the school yard. They dug a berm in a huge circle to hold the creek water as it froze into a skating surface. I took my skates to school so I could skate at noon hour.

Ronnie, a careless older boy, ran onto the ice with a broom and rammed it between my legs as I skated. I screamed in outrage that anyone would do that to me, but no one told him not to. I heard him laugh as he ran away to terrorize some other girl. Some people in the village said he was "slow," and maybe he was, but he was a bully too.

I'd never had to deal with bullies in the suburban schools I'd been to before - but in the country, the bigger boys would grab me, push me to the ground and shove my face into the snow – face washing they called it - until I thought I was going to suffocate. The snow was hard and rough with ice, and scraped my face until I cried with frustration.

One recess, Philip Loucks was going down the hill on a sled and another boy jumped on him and knocked him backwards. His head hit the icy hill with a "crack" and when he went back into the school, he couldn't remember anything. Denny Anderson walked him home but no one was there, so Philip lay down and slept. When his mother came home from work, kids coming out of the school told her what had happened. She rushed home and woke him every two hours all that night. I guess in those days, first aid knowledge was not common in country schools, because the Teacher should have gotten help for him as soon as it happened. Luckily, Philip had a hard head and lived to tell me the story many years later.

Perhaps most of these boys turned out all right, but some didn't. Ronnie ended up living and working with the Teacher. Ricky Anderson, anxious and awkward, ended up many years later helping the Teacher with chores and going with him to singles' dances to meet women. Al, the big boy who had pushed Philip and intimidated the younger children in the school, including me, was on the verge of being fired from his job several times.

Chapter 13
Cathy's Parents Listened To Her

When I put out notices on various Ontario village Facebook sites—Orono, Bowmanville, Newcastle, Newtonville—anywhere I thought former classmates might be living—I found Cathy Spry. Ironically, I was already "friends" with her husband, who had ridden the school bus to high school with me.

Cathy and I "met up" on Facebook chat. Despite all the passing years, she still resembled that small, cute, dark-haired girl I remembered. She shared her memories freely with me.

As we talked about the time she was molested by the Teacher, and her life after she left our village, I felt an immediate kinship with her. She thought child molestation should be brought out into the open, talked about, not hidden as it had been when we were children.

When I was a child, my mother told me that the Teacher had touched Cathy, but I didn't know the nature of what had happened or that there had been two incidents. She explained.

She had to go to the washroom during school hours, so she came downstairs from the Junior room. When she got to the washroom door, it was closed—someone was already in there, so she waited in the cloakroom. Mr. Pollard had obviously seen her because he crossed the downstairs classroom, where we children were working on our lessons, to the cloakroom, and then followed her into the washroom after the other child came out. He locked the door and said he was going to "help" her. She ran to the door, unlocked it, and ran back up the stairs to her classroom.

Another day after school the Teacher put his hand up her dress when she was singing, standing next to the school piano. Cathy told me she was startled and went home and told her mother. She remembers this being in the Spring of 1958, in the first year after I started Leskard School. To this day, she said, she can't stand beside a piano and sing.

Though I didn't remember these incidents, I must have been in the classroom when Pollard crossed the room to follow Cathy into the washroom. It bothered me that things happened right under my nose. I'd had to wait until I was an adult to learn the extent of his boldness when he molested, or attempted to molest, girls.

Cathy's parents took her out of school and called the police. They gathered in the Spry's living room and explained to the officers what had happened.

The officer said, "Let's be clear here. What the Teacher did is wrong and illegal, but no court will take a child's word against an adult."

Cathy remembered her mother protesting, "He touched our daughter! He followed her into the girls' washroom. Said he wanted to 'help' her. Luckily Cathy ran out of there. Otherwise, what would he have done? And this wasn't the only incident. He put his hand up her skirt when she stood to sing while he played the piano."

"Were there witnesses?"

"In the washroom, no. The piano incident was after school. There were other children sitting there but they weren't close enough to the piano to see anything."

"I understand. But the police can't do anything if no adult saw what went on."

"Well, he doesn't do any of this when there's an adult there, does he? What are we supposed to do?"

"Make sure your daughter knows not to stay in after school or at recess."

As I listened to Cathy tell her story, I realized two things. The police hadn't offered her or her parents very practical advice when the Teacher was also inappropriate during school hours. And it was Cathy's responsibility to keep herself safe.

"And she shouldn't be alone with him. Go to the school. Tell him that. Threaten him. Make sure he knows you're serious. No one will stop you."

Cathy was out of school for about a month. Finally, her mother brought her back to school before morning class. Mrs. Spry approached the Teacher, her face red with anger. She reached out both her hands toward the collars on his suit, but he backed away. She stood with her face only inches from his and yelled, "You are never to touch my daughter again! Don't ask her to stay after school or to stay in for recess, because she's not going to."

The Teacher said nothing. Cathy told me how much in awe of her mother she was as she "stood so strong she was scary." Mrs. Spry left the classroom with Cathy, who stayed outside in the playground until the morning bell rang.

Cathy's mother was very proactive and spoke to other girls in the village who had been molested by Pollard, but could only act on behalf of her own daughter. Cathy told me that her parents thought mine were "on her side," so she was surprised to learn that my mother didn't think my experience with the Teacher bothered me. Cathy's father often referred to the inaction of the village residents—those he called "those Leskardians."

The Spry family immediately began to search for a new house—far away from the village. Cathy's parents assured her that she wouldn't have to return to Leskard School in the fall, even if she had to go to Richmond Hill and live with her cousin in order to go to school.

Cathy told me her mother also talked with Reverend Long, another person who, because of his position as minister in the Orono, Kirby, and Leskard churches, was prominent in the village. Outside the Leskard village United Church—the same church I stayed in all these years later when I returned to the village to do my research—she approached him after a Sunday service and asked if they could talk privately.

Reverend Long had initially seemed so genuinely interested, Mrs. Spry felt herself relax. She explained to him that no one was paying attention to her concerns about the Teacher and she really hadn't known what to do. However, as soon as she told him what the issue was, his attitude immediately changed. He protested that Mr. Pollard was a "local boy," so he was not going to do anything. Mrs. Spry told Cathy that the reverend was "clearly uncomfortable" talking about such issues and he would rather not talk about, or do anything about, the situation.

In my various interviews, I heard several more unflattering reports about Reverend Long and his career as a village minister, but they didn't relate to Pollard and his activities, so I will let them rest.

After trying to get Rev. Long to listen to her, Mrs. Spry went outside the church, took a deep breath of fresh air, and vowed, *That's the last time I ever enter this church.* When she was an elderly woman, she told her daughter Cathy that, at the time, she felt completely alone.

Cathy and her family moved out of Leskard when she was nine—the summer after Mr. Pollard's activities came to light. They moved to Maple Grove.

After I finished Leskard School, I went to Clarke High School; Cathy went to Bowmanville High School. I started university; she studied nursing.

I valued being able to talk with her—the girl who alerted a whole village to the evil that was occurring. Being heard, validated, was so important to me on this journey. I appreciated Cathy's openness—she displayed so much confidence in contrast to myself, I wondered if that was due to her parents' response to their daughter. She said, "My parents listened to me."

She and I had both sought therapy to deal with our reactions to the past, though our situations were very different. As she grew, Cathy felt guilty for what she saw as "making her parents move" out of the small, seemingly idyllic village where her grandparents lived—but her parents didn't hold her responsible. They were the adults. They acted to shelter their daughter, while all the other children remained in the school. My parents not only sent me back to school after the initial uproar about the Teacher, they also sent my sister. After that, they only rarely referred to it and never discussed why they had made the decision they did.

I closed the computer screen after my call with Cathy and quickly jotted down notes so I would remember what she'd told me. A calmness came over me as I remembered the little girl who had exposed the issue of child abuse for all the village to see. As I had with Jill, I felt relief that I shared this history with another woman, a fellow student who might know how I'd felt when the Teacher violated me. But that is where the similarity between her story, and mine and Jill's ended.

Cathy said, quoting Hilary Clinton, "'It takes a village' to raise children, but not this village—they all looked the other way. My parents listened. They believed me. They protected me."

I so wanted to be able to say the same thing about my parents.

Chapter 14
What Happened To Me

Shortly after the village began to talk about what had happened to Cathy Spry, my mother called me into our bathroom. She sat on the edge of a chair. Perhaps some things are easier when discussed in a bathroom, or maybe she didn't want anyone else in the family to hear.

"Cathy Spry told her parents that the Teacher touched her. Her mother says she's talked to other girls that he's done this to. Has that ever happened to you?"

I knew immediately what my mother meant. I looked down at the floor, and told her, "Yes."

I didn't look up to see my mother's reaction, but I heard a little tremble in her voice as she asked me to tell her.

I didn't want to say what had happened, but I had to. The words came out slowly. "When I went back to school after being away with the flu, the Teacher told me I'd missed the school nurse's visit." I paused. "He told me I had to stay in for recess so he could examine me like the nurse would have." At this point, I stopped, my stomach flip-flopping under my clothes, hoping I wouldn't have to tell her the rest.

"Then what?" she asked.

"He told me I had to go to the upstairs classroom with him while all the other kids went outside." I remembered walking up the stairs ahead of him. Aware that my skirt came to just above my knees.

I watched my mother's face to see how she was reacting. She encouraged me to continue.

"He sat on a chair at the back of the classroom. Then he took out a pen and some papers that had spaces on them to be filled out. He told me to stand next to him."

"Okay, what happened then?" My mother had the same tone of voice she used when I'd done something wrong. I realized then that something shameful had happened. I didn't look at her.

After a bit more hesitation, I continued, "First he felt my arms and wrote something on the papers. Then he slid his hand under my skirt, slowly up the inside of my leg."

I couldn't say the next part... that he'd flattened his hand on my skin and that his hand went almost to my panties.

I didn't tell my mother I'd held my breath and stared intently at the clock on the wall, waiting until he finished with me. "Then he said I could go outside for the rest of the recess period."

My Mother's first response was not, "How did you feel?" or "Come here and let me put my arm around you," but rather, "Did you write the date down in your diary?"

Maybe. Not sure. I went up to my room to get my diary with the puffy red vinyl cover and a picture of a young girl casually holding a diary. The one my parents had given me for Christmas, 1959, when I was nearly ten and in grade five. I flipped through the pages, looking to see, and then showed my mother. No, I'd written nothing about what happened to me that day.

Why wouldn't I have written down something as startling as being touched in this way by my Teacher? Because it was unpleasant like going to the dentist? Something I just had to put up with, like the move our family had made to the country, to a strange school, away from my best friend? Like Mom screaming at me that I shouldn't be playing with silly paper dolls? At the time, it didn't seem any more hurtful than those things.

No one had warned me not to let anyone touch me like that. I'd been told not to take rides with strangers—but not what could happen if I did. Besides, the Teacher wasn't a stranger. I'd been told what to do if I walked home and lightning and thunder began to strike. I knew enough not to stand under a tree but instead to lie down in the middle of a field, though not precisely when I should do that. But not what to do if an adult ran his hand up my leg. Perhaps if I had been warned, I would have known that the Teacher was lying when he said I'd missed the nurse's visit and he needed to examine me. But I was so young, it never occurred to me that a teacher would lie to me, and I never thought of defying any teacher. Perhaps I just didn't pay attention to the feelings I had that told me what he did to me was wrong.

My mother took my diary from me. She wanted times and dates, but I felt angry and could only say, "If he touches Bonnie, I'll kill him." Perhaps those were the words I wanted her to say about me.

Like Cathy Spry, my younger sister Bonnie and I didn't go to school for the next few weeks. My Mother wanted to see what was going to happen to the Teacher. I heard her mumbled conversations on the phone with the school inspector. I knew that neighbours were gossiping at the corner General Store. Mom told me that the Teacher's father was on the school board. There were denials about any wrongdoing. She was disgusted with the "ignorant country people" who didn't seem to care who taught their children.

"He was let go from another school for doing the same things," my Mother said. But why did she tell me this? I couldn't do anything about it except be even more upset that people knew what he did to little girls but put him into our school anyway. Years later I found out that possibly he hadn't taught at any other school before ours, but back then, that was one of the rumours going around.

Though a few more girls were taken out of school by their parents, most kept going to class. Tillie Anderson went to the school to yell at the Teacher and threaten him because he molested her daughter. But some people just didn't see what all the fuss was about.

My mother called me into the living room for another discussion. It was out in the open now. She explained what the school inspector had told her. "In order to get rid of the Teacher, we'd have to write a report of what happened and then you'd have to go to a courtroom and tell a judge."

Okay I thought, with a feeling I now know was relief. Someone was going to do something.

But then she said, "That would be too traumatic for you."

Perhaps she was told by the Inspector that, in the fifties, courts rarely took the word of a child against an adult. Also, multiple cases of abuse didn't impact the court—each case would be judged separately, if at all. It was simply inconceivable, in those days, that a teacher, a Principal even, an upstanding professional man from a good family, would ever do such a thing.

Instead, my mother sent my sister and I back to school. Her advice to me, at ten years of age: "Just make sure you're never in a room alone with him again." When she said this, she must have believed the Teacher *would* try to touch me again, otherwise why warn me? But she was also stating very clearly that she and my father were not going to help me. I wanted my parents, my mother and father, to do something like Cathy's parents had, but they didn't. I had to protect myself.

From that time, my parents didn't feel like safety to me, like home.

* * *

My parents, like many people, assumed that pedophiles (an adult who has sexual fantasies about or engages in sexual acts with a prepubescent child) would hide their actions, but as perpetrators become more used to the students and what they can get away with, they take chances—do it openly or do it in such a way that they could easily be found out if someone only took the time to look.

Cathy Spry's abuse took place during school hours, a couple of feet from our senior room where the students were doing their school work, and after school, in front of other children. Our Teacher had girls sit on his lap in front of the whole class while he looked at their school work. He was not concerned that he would get into trouble.

Miss Cobbledick, the Junior teacher, had taken the rumours to her supervisor, but was told that, without an adult witness, she could only warn the girls not to stay in at recess or lunch hour—leaving it up to the students themselves to stop the Teacher.

In Calgary, a teacher at John Ware Junior High school was finally charged and arrested in 2021 after twenty years of abusing as many as two hundred female students. There were signs from the beginning of his teaching career. His abuse was often in the open. Complaints were made to school officials, but no action was taken. Just as in our situation.

* * *

When I returned to school weeks after Cathy Spry's revelation, the Teacher took me aside at recess as I lined up to get a drink at the fountain.

"You were away for a few weeks."

"Yes," I said, already beginning to feel very uncomfortable.

"Why?"

I could feel my face burn red. My mother hadn't prepared me for his questions—perhaps she didn't think he would do such a thing. I just stood there. After a few seconds, he smirked and walked away. His message was clear to me—he had won. My parents and I couldn't or wouldn't do anything about him.

* * *

Maybe it was my fault. At the time the Teacher touched me, I didn't tell my mother. I hadn't even written it down in my diary. When my Mother said I had to return to school, I didn't argue and protest that I wouldn't go back. I was a good girl. I did what I was told. I didn't say anything. Also, I was torn—I loved school, loved learning, loved achieving—but that joy was stolen from me.

I learned that it is easier to shut down than to be brave or defiant. It becomes even harder to be brave when you are not aware you have choices. My ability to see choices and to actually choose was shut down.

My mother took phenobarbital to cope with her loneliness and isolation, but that drug also took her away from us as surely as my Dad's beer-drinking took him away. I had to withstand the pain of my parents' decision for me to return to school, but I didn't have drugs or alcohol to numb me. Still, I had to have a way of coping, to calm myself. Each day when I got home from school—on good weather days—I rode my bicycle back into the fields. When I got back to the tree plantation about a mile behind my house, and the small irrigation pond dug to water the tiny trees, I stopped, put my bike down, and lay flat in the long grass to stare up into the sky, Then I was able to breathe, relax, and let my tension flow out into the ground. Of course, at the time, I didn't really know what I was doing. I just knew I could slip between the tall blades of grass and sing at the top of my lungs. Sing my favourite songs like "The Twelfth of Never" by Johnny Mathis and "Lonesome Town" by Ricky Nelson.

Though previously I'd worried about my sister, like my mother, I learned to just ignore what was happening, and carry on. What more could I do? Nothing. At first, when we moved to the country, Bonnie and I were necessary playmates. We had no one else. I would reach across the abyss between our beds in our home to hold her small hand and tell her the story of the Three Bears. Night after night she would ask me to do this. It comforted us both. Our bedroom was not so dark then, the loneliness not so harsh. Yet I barely remember Bonnie in the years I was in grades six to eight, even though she walked with me to and from school every morning and every evening. Years later Bonnie screamed at me that I was never a sister to her. And perhaps she was right. As I think back, there are many times I don't even remember her being there.

The longer we lived in the country, the more numb and "absent" I became. I know now I was in a form of denial about what was happening, so I could survive emotionally.

I was in the Teacher's class for grades four, five, six, seven, and eight. Five years. And five years is a very long time in the life of a child. Though he never touched me again in exactly the same way, I grew into adolescence under my Teacher's watchful eyes. Bonnie, too, spent five years in the Teacher's class after I went to high school. Many years later, she told me that she, too, had been molested.

Chapter 15
The Village Knows About The Teacher

On January fifteenth, 1959, ten days after my tenth birthday, I wrote the following in my diary: *Today Margie screamed at Mr. Pollard and I don't blame her. Margie and Mindy walked out of the school. The Teacher wanted Margie, a girl older than me who sat in the next row, to stay in after school. She yelled at him, 'I'm not staying in so you can pull my pants down!'*

I looked at my diary and felt the disgust that, as a ten-year-old child, I couldn't articulate. I had written about my classmate yelling out in class about being molested by our pedophile Teacher on the same page I'd written about going to skating practice to get ready for the Orono Winter Carnival. I was living in two worlds. One was the world of adult sexuality that I was too young to really understand. The other was a normal childhood with skating lessons and school work.

As Cathy Spry told me all these years later, "You would have to be in the class with Pollard in order to really understand what it was like."

What it was like could be as simple as when the girl from the junior class forgot to take her ball out with her for recess. She ran up the stairs to her classroom to get it, opened the door, and the Teacher yelled, "Shut the door and get out!" She glimpsed him, face red with anger, his legs splayed out, sitting on a chair with a girl on his lap. She hurried back down the steps and out the door.

That day, when Margie had screamed her outrage, silence descended, pens were suspended in midair, every eye on the Teacher. He had been caught off guard, and it showed on his round, bloated face. He squirmed in his chair behind his big desk. Snickered. I could see the glint of sunlight on his misshapen front tooth. He likely thought no one would have the courage to yell out that he touched the girls.

He looked around at every child, "I don't know what she's talking about."

At that, Margie and Mindy, the girl who sat next to Margie, rose from their desks and walked out of the classroom. Margie was brave—much braver than me. I am still in awe of what she did.

That night, I wrote in my diary that I couldn't *"expect him to admit it"* and *"He needs to be put out of the school."* After Margie and Mindy came back to school the next day, I again wrote in my diary, *"I hope we get a new teacher."*

The Teacher wasn't afraid to continue blurring the lines between acceptable and unacceptable behaviour. Coming to my desk to see how I was progressing with a reading assignment meant him lifting the edge of my dress to admire, and ask questions about, my new crinoline. I tried to keep my eyes on my notebook as he did this—afraid to say anything.

If a girl was told to stay after school, she never knew if the request was legitimate or an excuse for the Teacher to get her alone, the doors locked. The question was always there—like the stale odour of rotten vegetables that lingers even after the garbage bin has been cleaned. Even when the Teacher was doing ordinary things, I could smell the rot floating in the classroom, taking up space. In and out, I breathed the same air as he did, so every day I inhaled the uncertainty of my existence.

* * *

An emergency meeting was held, though I didn't know that at the time. Joan Lewis, a woman who'd gone to school with the Teacher, described the public meeting that was held at the school, though she hadn't been there herself. From her description, I have put together what happened.

Each country school had three members of the community on the school board—all men, and usually men from old established families in the area. The ones that felt they had the right to positions of authority. In our village, it was Earl McDonald, the store owner, George Pollard, the Teacher's father, and Mr. Scott, who hailed from a family that had always had a farm here. Three men who could be counted on to stick together and not "rock the boat." They must have met before the village meeting to decide who would speak and what they would say about the Teacher.

Apparently, many villagers attended, those with children and those without. This was more excitement than many had seen in a long time. Cathy Spry's parents were there and stood to tell their daughter's story. They had no hesitation speaking out. "Our daughter was touched by the Teacher. For heaven's sake, he followed her into the girls' washroom."

They were challenged, "Who saw this happen? Any adults?"

"Well, there weren't any adults there. It was during class time."

"You're trying to tell us," the Teacher's father spoke slowly, emphasizing every word, "that the Teacher went into the washroom after your daughter in front of all the rest of the students?" He paused and then said, "I find that... very hard to believe. No one would be that obvious if they were going to do something wrong."

"Our daughter told us what happened."

"She is a young child. Only eight years old. Hasn't she ever told fibs before?" Many of those present laughed.

"Other girls have been touched, too," she defended.

Mrs. Spry had looked around at those she thought were her friends and neighbours. Many looked the other way when she caught their eye. Some sat defiantly, like the Bayleys and Mrs. McDonald. No one supported her. I imagine that, if my parents had attended, they would just have sat there, taking it all in, occasionally whispering to each other. My mother would never tell my story, and my Dad would never have allowed her to, anyway. Not in public.

Finally, a villager rose, red-faced, stiff, and yelled out, "He's one of our own. We have to take care of our own."

Cathy Spry's grandparents had a farm just up the hill from the general store, on the corner of Ball's Road and Concession 8, so the Spry family was also "one of our own," but that was ignored.

Various comments went back and forth about the Sprys leaving the village and information about what the school inspector had said—that no one was going to take the word of children over an adult.

Murmurings in the crowd revealed annoyance that anyone would talk about such things. Most who attended felt this would all die down and everything would go back to normal. They wanted to believe that this "fuss" was all the result of silly little girls with bigger imaginations than sense—

not to blame them, after all, they're children. Perhaps parents shouldn't take these things so seriously. This could have been a very damaging situation—they could have mistakenly accused a talented teacher of something that was impossible for him to have done. Perhaps they felt lucky to have him teaching in the village school. Children were being taught music and singing—by "one of our own."

Many villagers simply couldn't believe this would happen in their village, so everyone counted on this upset just being forgotten. But my interviews, all these years later, had shown me that no one had forgotten.

Denying the children's experience meant that the children were seen as liars. I was a liar. Jill was a liar. Cathy Spry was a liar. Our very reality was denied while the Teacher was believed.

Though we children may not have understood the Teacher's motivations, his actions were obvious to us—but his true character was unknown to the villagers who refused to face reality.

* * *

In thinking back, the fact Mr. Pollard had not only been hired as a teacher in our village school but had also been appointed Principal right out of Teachers' College, likely had a lot to do with his father being on the school board—nepotism alive and well in Leskard. So, of course he was going to be supported by his father. George Pollard would have had to admit he made a mistake when he hired his son, and that was not going to happen.

Also, several I interviewed suggested that Mr. McDonald, the store owner, had his own concerns which may have been more important than finding out the truth about the Teacher. He couldn't afford to lose the Pollard family grocery business or the business of those who might shop elsewhere because of their relationship with the Pollards, so he didn't say anything against the Teacher. This was not a hornet's nest he wanted to stir up. Memories are long in small villages, and ways to make a living, few.

In addition, McDonald just didn't want any fuss. He didn't want the village to get a reputation. To be seen as a bad place. A place where things like child molestation could happen. In good families.

Many of the women in the village likely thought back to when they were young. There were men their mothers told them to stay away from. That's how things were done back then. No police, just keep it in the village, handle it themselves.

* * *

In contrast, my Nana, widowed in her late thirties, ran a boarding house in Oshawa, and one man, Burt, had been living in her house for many years. He was a carpenter and, when I was young, he built a small dolls' clothes wardrobe for me, complete with a clothes rail, and drawer at the bottom.

One day when we were visiting Nana, my mother yelled, "Where is your little brother?"

I looked around, up the stairs, in the bathroom, and out in the back garden.

Then Nana flew across the dining room, flung open the French doors to the living room and screamed, "What are you doing with him?"

"Nothing, I'm not doing anything," Burt said in protest.

Nana grabbed my brother out of his arms and didn't give Burt time to explain—she had seen enough.

"Get out of here. Get upstairs and pack your things. You are not to come back here."

We never saw him again. That was how Nana dealt with someone who touched my brother.

After my mother became aware of the Teacher's actions, she told me she didn't want to shake his hand. I guess she didn't want to touch the hand that went up little girls' dresses. The fingers that had touched them. That was her form of protest.

* * *

The spring I was ten, I was diagnosed with rheumatic fever and told to lie still for six weeks. I stayed home from school, away from the Teacher. Illness let me escape for a short time. Years later a blood test revealed that I'd never had rheumatic fever at all—a wrong diagnosis. Perhaps my body knew I just needed to be safe, for at least a little while.

* * *

In the 1950s, parenting in Southern Ontario generally consisted of telling children what the rules were, what was expected of them, what was taboo, what was acceptable—and what punishment would be meted out if the rules weren't followed—the "sin" or religious guilt model of life. Most parents didn't see their job as listening to their children—in fact, listening might indicate that they didn't know what they were doing. For the most part, priests, teachers and parents weren't interested in what children were thinking or feeling— only what they were or weren't doing. (Rosemond, J. 2013)

My classmates and I were so young, so naïve, so easily led, so inexperienced—just as we'd been taught to be. And therefore, so easily manipulated. I felt wracked with guilt if I put a foot wrong. I did my best at school, got high marks, made my parents proud, and was eventually complimented by my high school teachers for what was seen as my "maturity." I was told to be obedient at school—and that had set me up to obey the Teacher when he had told me to come upstairs with him. Most children lived with the certainty that those with more power than they had, would wield that power. Families like the Sprys who moved out of our village when their daughter was molested, were the exception—they listened to their child.

Chapter 16
Death In The Village

In 1959, when I was ten, the second summer after we'd moved to the country, I still didn't know all the surrounding roads, the landmarks, the homes, and farms. We still shopped at the same grocery stores in Oshawa, and visited my nana on Saturdays.

My mother, sister, and I were returning from shopping and had just turned from Taunton Road onto Leskard Road that ran north to the village, when a car came toward us. The driver motioned to my mother to stop and the two cars blocked the road, each facing the opposite direction.

"There's been an accident at your place," the man said to my Mom.

When we'd left our house in the morning, a group of men and older boys were there, cutting hay and baling it in our fields.

Her eyes opened wide as she asked, "What kind of accident?" possibly afraid that my father was hurt.

"Someone's been killed."

"What!"

I sat in the front seat next to my mother and listened to the news.

"Yes, Allan Martin. A boy from the village."

I remembered him—he was about three years older than me, in grade eight. Dead? No, that was impossible.

"What happened?" she whispered. Maybe thinking that my sister and I wouldn't hear—or understand.

While the haying was going on, some of the boys were fooling around. One was driving a tractor. Two others were on the tractor's fenders, each boy sitting on one fender. One of them was Allan. The man paused, and then continued the story. Ronnie, that boy from the 7th line? He was driving. You know those three-wheeled tractors. He drove one of the back wheels up onto a bale of hay and it tipped. The whole thing came down on Allan. He didn't suffer—gone in a matter of seconds. Stupid, really. It was an accident. But it's a mess. The ambulance was there when I left.

He advised my mother to wait a bit before going home. Let them clear everything away. The man waited a few moments to let the news sink in and then drove away.

One of the boys from my school, dead? Ronnie, one of the boys who bullied us at school, responsible?

"Okay," Mom said to us, "Let's go into Orono. I have to pick up a few things I forgot. I'll turn the car around and we can go to the drug store and the IGA."

Gone. He was gone. Still just a boy. I really didn't know him. Wasn't friends with him. But I knew who he was. Older than me but not by a lot. Dead.

From that point on I felt odd—upset—going into the small field behind our barn. That was where it had happened. Of course, I didn't know exactly where, but it was in that field. I saw the bales of hay, ones just left in the field rather than thrown up onto the hay wagon. The larger field had been cleared of bales, but not that one. To this day, it feels strange. The unthinkable had happened there, in our field.

One of Jill's brothers had been on the other fender. If the tractor had fallen the other way, he would have died, not

Allan Martin. But her brother was still alive, as was the big boy who had been too careless, too silly to know what would happen if he drove one of the wheels of the tractor up onto a bale. It was just a bit of fun—like joy riding, but with a tractor. Fun, like when he terrorized the smaller children at school. Boys will be boys. An accident. But one boy died.

* * *

I opened my eyes, sat straight up in bed, put my slippers on just before my feet hit the cold linoleum, then walked across the bedroom to stand at the window. No stars or moon pierced the dark. I could see less than a quarter of a mile away, to the next farm. Usually I saw the barn on that farm, the house and all the outbuildings hiding behind it. Until that night.

Oranges, yellows, and reds shimmered through the wobbly glass of my window—installed in the 1840s when our house had been built. Flames licked around the edges of the wooden walls standing on top of the stone base of the barn. As I watched, the roof of the barn cracked in two and fell within the walls, the flames escaping into the night.

I heard my dad downstairs tell my mother he was driving over. Men were gathering around to watch the spectacle, smoke their cigarettes, and speculate as to the cause of the fire. There was nothing much anyone could really do.

Two water trucks drove up as close to the barn as possible. The drivers must have stuck their hoses into the creek deep in the valley to pump water into the tanks at the back of the trucks, but there were no power hoses to get enough water onto the barn to make a dent in the burning.

The volunteer fire brigade threw pails-full haphazardly at the edges of the fire. No one could get close.

Behind the glass of my window, I could hear nothing. Nothing of the men. Nothing of the water trucks. Nothing of the crackling of the fire. Nothing of the crying of the cows, the singeing of their fur, the burning of their eyes as they beat their heads against the wooden gates of their stalls. Nothing of the frantic squawking of the chickens as their feathers smashed against the roof of their coop in the basement of the barn. I could hear nothing—but I watched.

Eventually I went back to bed, to an uneasy sleep.

I woke as usual to the ring of the alarm clock on the nightstand. No way to avoid the inevitable. Though I knew it was pointless, I took time to choose clothes so the Teacher wouldn't look at me that way. The image of the burning barn still lingered in my head.

My sister and I walked to school on the dirt road that ran beside the burned barn. I slowed my footsteps so I could see the huge field-stone wall that made up the lowest part. Dad had told me that it was built of glacier-deposited granite boulders gathered from fields over a hundred years before when the farm was first established, just like that part of our barn.

The roof of the barn was gone. What remained of the top floor was black, the misshapen charcoal boards no longer making sense. Most had collapsed into the stone shell beneath.

The fire was out but the smell had begun. Each morning and afternoon after that, as we walked past the wreckage, the aroma grew—at first like that of a giant campfire, then slowly becoming more ugly and pungent.

Had the animals screamed as they died—for I'd no doubt they'd died. I'd smelled dead animals before—mice and squirrels huddling behind the walls of our house, taking their last breaths after they'd eaten the poison Dad put out to get rid of them. I could almost gauge how long they'd been dead, and how long our family would have to endure the smell of their deadness, by the strength of the odour. So, I knew the dead smell. But in this barn, death was not boxed up tidily behind walls. It was bigger, more frightening, more immediate, right beside the road, animals killed by the fire. Dead animals in the burned barn.

I had no idea how long the smell would last.

When it rained, gruesome death ran right out onto the road, creating grey-brown puddles with thick foam floating on the top. Not water my sister or I would splash in or sail small boats on.

My chest tightened each time we walked by. My throat burned, though the fire was out. I looked back towards the barn, afraid to move—afraid of what I might see.

Why hadn't anyone taken the animals out of the barn and buried them? Was I the only one who could smell this? The stench continued for months, the whole of the summer. Why wasn't this dealt with? When the foulness was there for all to smell. As it was in the school we were forced to attend. Why didn't anyone do anything?

Chapter 17
Village Life

In some ways, our village was like so many other rural communities. There were happy times and bad, good, caring, intelligent people, and those who were mean-spirited, prejudiced and backward in their thinking. Families in the village were mainly of two groups—those whose ancestors went back generations to the original settlers, and newcomers like us. But the newcomers were also in two distinct groups—those who fit in and those who were different.

As a child, I had no idea of the networks—the mycelium—that tied together the various families in the village, which my family and I weren't part of. Our relatives were miles away in Oshawa and Kingston—we were the outsiders, related to no one local.

Many people were family to others both in the village and on the surrounding farms—sisters, brothers, aunts, uncles, cousins. The Loucks family was interconnected, Brian and his family were related to Aunt Jenny Watson, the Chaters, and others like Charlie Campbell, a friend of my father and mother. Joan Gimblett had been born in the village into a family of twelve children who were all nieces and nephews of the Davy family, whose farm my family had bought. Jill's family was related to the Pollards and another farming family on the 7th Concession.

Philip Loucks was three grades ahead of me. I remembered him from school, so I contacted him via Facebook. He wrote back with lots to tell about his family. His father had moved to the village from Toronto for health reasons and started working on the farm just to the east of us. Philip's grandparents, and eventually three of his father's sisters, moved to the village.

Philip's father and grandparents bought sixty-five acres, a barn, and chicken coop east of the village—the house on the property had burned down. The family lived in the chicken coop (cleaned out and fixed up but with no running water) and used an outhouse. They added a cistern to catch water and in a few years added two bedrooms and a bathroom—with one of those chemical toilets like we had.

Life was hard then. The family had a pair of horses Philip's father used to work in the gravel pit just north of the village to earn extra money. Their six cows were milked by hand. They separated the milk and sold the cream, like the Chaters and other farmers in the area. Philip had to walk the cows down to the stream in the winter, break the ice, and let them drink. At that point, his mother said they had to put in running water!

The story of Philip's father digging their well is one of grit and determination. After the local dowser told them where to dig, he started digging by hand—a three-foot-circumference well. His mother and older brother ran a windless to bring the dirt up from the hole. After a full summer of digging, their father reached fifty feet and still there was no water. He gave up—at that depth there was so little air in the shaft, he couldn't breathe. Luckily, it didn't cave in on him. A well driller was called in and hit water at eighty-five feet. Our well was also very deep. Like the Loucks family, we lived on the top of a hill—though on the opposite side of the deep village valley.

In time, the family moved down the road to another house while Philip's father tore down the chicken coop house, and, with no formal training, designed and built an entirely new house for the family. From Philip who, as a boy, raised hens and sold the eggs, to his parents, they were a family that survived on their own know-how.

Philip, his sister, and brother had a bobsled they raced down their hill east of the village all the way to the bottom of the valley where the general store stood. One day, they were racing someone on another sled and a car came over the school hill. The two sleds split around it and carried on down to the store. Thinking back all those years ago, I knew my mother would never have allowed me to do that. The Loucks children had freedom I could only dream of.

Because Philip was older than me, he started at the village school before the Teacher came. The school only occupied the downstairs room then, with all eight grades crammed in together. At first, he was taught by Mrs. Ward, a tyrant. Teachers in the early fifties were rulers of their kingdoms—the classroom—and if you got a bad one, little was done. Mrs. Ward had a heavy ball of string she would throw at students if they misbehaved, and she hit children with the wooden pointer. When Mrs. Ward left, she was replaced for a short while by Miss Ard, a teacher everyone loved. Philip's family even invited her for dinner.

When I was in Leskard school, I always thought of Philip as a nice boy, so it was heart-warming for me to read so many years later, in his Facebook note to me, about his family working hard, laughing, and allowing their children a normal upbringing.

* * *

One of the houses in the village was owned by a couple from Toronto. The Holmes were school teachers who only came on weekends and summer holidays. To me, they were exotic—they lived in that faraway city that felt like a mecca to me—and were well-educated. Every so often they would bring a box of shells, or rocks and minerals, to the school for the children to see. On Hallowe'en, they took pictures of us children in our costumes and then showed us the slides on the following Hallowe'en. We would sit quietly in the dark, and see how we had looked the year before.

Hallowe'en was magical to me—the only time I was allowed to wander with village children after dark. Families often made their own Hallowe'en treats—Mrs. Gimblett made toffee apples, Mrs. Glenn popcorn balls. Mrs. McDonald at the General Store handed out tiny bags of penny candy.

I remember the year we were walking back down the hill toward the general store, when Al, Bill, and Ronnie came running along the road, hollering, "Hey you'll never guess what we just did! Pushed over old man Smith's outhouse!" Then they laughed and raced off.

While I didn't like vandalism, I was impressed by the outrageous boldness of these boys.

Children rarely made the long walk up the hills to our house for Hallowe'en because we lived so far out of the village, so my mother sent candy to school to hand out to the children when we had our class party. She often sent licorice pipes—those black, sticky, thick, sickeningly sweet treats that she liked, but I hated. Also, for all our class parties, she sent egg or salmon salad sandwiches, which the children devoured.

The girls in my class thought Mom was wonderful. One day I sat in the car waiting for her to pick up the mail at the General Store. I saw her come out the door and pause to talk and laugh with some of my classmates standing on the store porch. The next day in school Janie said to me, "It must be wonderful to have a mother that is so much fun, so friendly." For a minute, I wondered who she was talking about, and then, with a sharp pain in my chest, wondered why I never saw that side of my mother.

* * *

One of the activities we children all liked was the school nature walk. The Teacher would lead us up and down roads around the village and sometimes we would collect things. Bits of moss, stones, and branches to put on the windowsills, flowers to put into jars to decorate the classroom. One time a cecropia moth came back with us to the school. It landed on one boy's hand and stayed there. He carried it back and we put it in an open jar in the class. It would fly around a bit and land on the frame of one of the windows—perhaps a sign he wanted out? Eventually he flew out the door and back to the wilderness.

Some of the nature walks took us past empty buildings. One old farmhouse stood on a hill not far off the road. Jill and I decided to go back to it the following weekend.

We walked up the road discussing whether we were too nervous to go into the old abandoned house.

"Who lived there?"

"I don't know." Jill said, "Even though we've lived here ever since I was born."

"There could be ghosts of old farm people who died," I said. "But if it looks dangerous or rickety, we can't go in."

She looked at me. "My dad would kill me if I fell through some floor boards."

We approached the house slowly, perhaps afraid of what might pop out at us from the windows or doors. The front door was propped open with a rock and a quick look inside revealed old pop bottles, a small dead fire in the middle of the floor, cigarette butts. Clearly some people had used it as a hide-out, a club house, or just a place to hang out. I could see stairs leading up to the second floor but most steps were broken and not worth risking our necks for. Instead, we walked around the outside of the house peeking into the windows, and didn't see much that was interesting— but there was still a feeling of uneasy excitement.

What do buildings hold? Memories? Spirits of the dead? The hopes and dreams of the ones who have gone before? All the emotions the families had, good and bad? We left to cross the fields that led back to Jill's house, kicking dry cow pies as we went.

Later that week, Jill and I started a wildflower sketching book. Along the sides of the school were lilac bushes— mauve and white—that smelled so beautiful in the late Spring, and bridal wreath spirea we would shake to loosen the small white petals that swirled around our heads like confetti. Our country school could have been so wonderful.

* * *

Our home was one mile west of the village school—I know because my mother told me. She must have paced it on the odometer of the car out of curiosity to see how far her children had to walk each morning and afternoon.

I often got to school just as the Teacher stopped ringing the hand bell or after the schoolyard emptied out—the children already in the classroom. Anxious to get there on time, I usually ran up the last hill to the school.

One day I ran across the baseball diamond and tripped. My knee scraped along the dirt, my lunch pail crashed to the ground, and I heard the glass inside my thermos bottle telling me I had no drink for lunch that day. Replacing the glass liner in my thermos was a tiresome regular event for my mother. I walked into the cloakroom with blood dripping down my leg into my sock, stopped into the washroom to get toilet paper to mop up the mess, and then went to my desk. Scabs on my legs were also a regular thing.

I didn't have the longest walk to school—Margie, the brave girl a grade ahead of me, lived on the farm further west and south of our home. I wasn't allowed to ride my bike to school—I guess my mother thought it was too dangerous—so if I were lucky enough to be walking to school at exactly the same time she was and she had her bicycle, she'd give me a ride.

I rode on the back of Margie's bike, down the steep hills covered with loose gravel—hair flying, lunch pail clutched in the hand that encircled her waist. Margie was obviously a very skilled bike rider. She steered her bicycle and kept it upright on the gravel road with me sitting on the seat while she stood to peddle. To this day, I can still see the hill stretching down in front of us—and have no idea what kept us from crashing. I would have caught hell—though I would never have called it that—if I'd had to show my mother the resultant injuries.

Maybe my mother had heard the story of Philip Loucks when he hadn't been so lucky on his bicycle. One summer day, he and another friend rode to visit his old teacher and her husband who lived north of the village. When he went down a steep hill, his front fender came off and wrapped around the wheel. He flew over the handlebars and dragged along the gravel road, ending up with sand and gravel-encrusted scrapes and blood—the hazards of bicycle riding in the country.

* * *

Each day after school, my job was to go into the general store that sat at the main village corner to pick up our mail before I started the walk home. The store stood at the bottom of the hill from the school—an easy downhill walk. Many of the children like Janie and Marilyn Gregory, Ricky and Leslie Anderson—lived in the village, so by the time we reached the store, they were almost home, while my walk had barely begun. The stop at the store was a welcome break before my long uphill trek.

Mona and Earl McDonald lived behind the long wooden counter of the village general store day and night, or so it seemed. Mrs. McDonald was short, and, like a plastic bobble-head, her grey helmet of waved hair seemed welded into place. Earl's form was thinner and taller, so he easily slipped around her in the confined space behind the counter. But they matched each other in their grim looks of determination. It was as though they had agreed decades before what their faces should look like, so there was less to decide each morning as they prepared to open the store for business.

When I went up to the counter, Mrs. McDonald walked over to the postal cubby holes, located the one that had our family name on it, and handed me our letters and bills.

I faced sweet temptations every time I stepped inside the store, so it should have been a magical place. Only glass separated me from the boxes of round black jawbreakers, orange candy corn, Black Jack gum, red wax lips, and pink marshmallows sugar-coated to resemble real strawberries. But, as with Hansel and Gretel, the way to the candy was through the witch that stood guard. I slid my pennies across the wooden counter to Mrs. McDonald and she got a tiny paper sack to house my few sweet treats—never altering her expression.

If I wanted my money to stretch further, I chose the orange and yellow candy corn that was three for a penny, rather than sweets that were a penny each. It was risky buying any during the week, though. I had to eat them before I got home so Mom wouldn't see them. I wasn't allowed to have much candy when I was growing up, so I guess I craved it even more. When I saved my allowance, I bought a ten-cent Superman or Mickey Mouse comic book or a twelve-cent Classics Illustrated, which had much more exciting stories. The big decision was whether I wanted the Classics Illustrated badly enough to spend the extra two cents, or whether I wanted more penny candy.

The new monthly comic book editions were displayed on a stand that went 'round and 'round so you could see all the selections. That carrousel held me mesmerized. As I set down my lunch box and reached out my hands to pick up one of the comic books, intending to flip through and see if it was worth my investment, Mr. McDonald cleared his throat in my direction. Mrs. McDonald was more direct, "Comic books are for people who buy them. Put it back."

The store was the centre of the "village telegraph." Hearsay and whispers took the place of a newspaper, though much of what was discussed would likely never make it into a normal news column. Information about villagers was passed on, commented on, and judged, vacation postcards read and discussed.

All the old biddies in the village and surrounding countryside counted up the months after any wedding, until the first child was born. When one of the young women in the village got married, she sent a postcard to her mother, knowing it would be read in the store. "Don't worry, my 'monthly visitor' arrived while on honeymoon."

My mom called it gossip. "I don't want you to say anything in the store—about anything!"

What Mom didn't realize was that no matter what we did, we were talked about anyway.

When I went into the store to collect the mail, villagers were hanging out, smoking and chatting. Once I walked into the store and the chatting stopped. I caught the words "those newcomers," as one man punched the arm of the man beside him. I wondered what he had been saying, while I went to the counter to ask for our mail. As I opened the door to leave, I could hear laughter behind me.

I knew that Mr. McDonald—a man one of my interviewees called a "prejudicial fart"—would look to see there was no one in the store who would object if he gossiped about the new family up the hill. As in other communities in Southern Ontario at that time, many people thought Catholics were strange, or worse. Despite the fact that no one knew what we Catholics said or did in our religion, they still believed it wasn't right. The general feeling among McDonald and others like him was that our family had come to the village—they didn't ask us to. We should do what they do.

And Dad was a foreman in General Motors, not on "the line" like other men in the village, adding to the myth that we thought we were better than everyone else.

* * *

Some days, if we kids were lucky, Mr. Robbins was at the store with his horse and buggy. "Come on, jump on the back if you want a ride up the hill." When our family moved to the country, he owned the next farm east, on the opposite side of the road from us.

Jill and I would climb into the back section of the buggy, where the trunks rode when people regularly travelled by carriage. It was a treat, though I'm sure I arrived home smelling a bit like horse and having eaten a lot of dust.

Most of the time, though, we walked up the hills to our homes.

* * *

One summer day after school, a group of children formed at the bridge over Wilmot Creek, the shallow creek that ran through the village. The cement bridge, built in 1952, five years before we moved to the village, had replaced the original wooden one. It enabled back-and-forth traffic from our side of the bridge to the other, attaching us to the village. We all went down to the creek to throw rocks into the water. Some of us were under the bridge and some were hidden by bushes when something came fluttering down. Someone had thrown some paper that landed on the rocks below. We waited for the person to leave, then crept over to what looked like a magazine.

One of the older boys, picked it up and started to turn the pages. I moved closer to see the pictures. One of the other boys laughed and said, "It's a nudie magazine."

I wanted to see. Pictures of women. Mostly undressed. Bare naked women. Bare legs. Bottoms—*derrières*, my mother would say—scarcely covered. I laughed and turned away, then ran up the bank of the creek toward the road. As I turned back one last time, Billy was ripping out the pages one by one and throwing them into the water. Bare breasts floated away as I turned to walk home.

The children who lived in the village dispersed to their homes, while Jill, her brothers, Margie, and I started our longer walk home.

* * *

When I was young, everything seemed huge. The hills from the village up to my home seemed enormous—especially in the month of June, when the heat lay silent and relentless. The gravel road was dusty and covered with stones, particularly in those last days before summer holiday. When cars drove by, the clouds of dust would get into my nose, my mouth, and into my hair, my shoes, my socks, and onto my dress. We children would try to walk on the side of the road in the grass, or in the ruts made by car tires, but if the grader had been by to smooth out the road, the gravel was spread across the road and into the ruts. Every step was a minefield of marble-like hazards under our shoes.

We trudged up the very first and steepest hill from the village, stopping occasionally to catch our breaths, until we could see right over the top of the hill to the big maple.

The trunk of the old maple was three children wide, topped by a crown of branches and leaves that spread from the road to the field. Under it was a huge boulder for our small group of children to perch on. I sat there to eat the candy strawberries my mother forbade. Today the old maple is only a memory—a stump and the rock are the only things remaining.

* * *

Before summer holiday started, we students spent the last few weeks of school getting entries ready for the Orono Fall Fair. Essays and poems were written, drawings and paintings completed during literature and art periods to be sent to the Fair committee for judging over the summer. They would be displayed at the fair in September. All the children in the classroom worked hard on the entries, as the first prize in many categories was one dollar. With an allowance of only twenty-five cents a week, this was much more money than I, and many of the other children, would ever see. When I won ten dollars from the Rotary Club for my page-long essay entitled "The Maple Tree," I could hardly believe how rich I was!

June was also the month when Physical Education consisted of practicing for field day, and playing baseball. The Teacher had obviously assessed my body and, as a result, said I should be able to shine in both baseball and high jump because I was tall for my age. But I was awkward and never good at sports.

My failure at any physical endeavour meant I endured embarrassment the whole month of June. We lined up to do high jump, long jump, and shot put to see who would represent our school at the township field day. Then we raced other children in our age group to see who was the fastest. My sister Bonnie was much better at sports than I was, even from an early age, so she came first in many of her competitions. I went to the field day, but was only entered in the girls' relay race because there had to be four girls in each age group on each team.

I was not much better at baseball, though I did try. Stuck out in left field, I couldn't do too much harm, but I remember the year I got hit in the face with the ball and my glasses ended up in pieces. After that, I was appointed the official scorekeeper—our school needed someone who would pay attention to the game and record the runs correctly, especially when we competed against other schools in the township.

No matter what activity was happening at school, I felt anxious most days, remembering what the Teacher had done to me and Cathy Spry. I couldn't do anything about any of it. He was my teacher for five years, my classmate Jill had him for all eight grades in elementary school. We were all stuck, trapped. But at the end of June each year, I was free. Summer days stretched ahead of me.

* * *

The month of June, as it creeps into early July, is strawberry season in southern Ontario. The days are long and sweltering. A farm a few miles away had acres and acres of strawberry plants planted in long straight rows. The summer I was eleven, Mom decided that she, my sister, and I would pick strawberries. We had to kneel on the straw-covered paths in between the rows, or bend down to give our knees a break, in order to earn seven cents for every quart we harvested.

We only picked in the mornings so the rest of the field could ripen for the next day's picking. Each day at noon, after tallying up our earnings, Mom and I took home one quart each of the huge red berries and each night Mom would make strawberry shortcake.

Mom used Bisquick, a boxed mix, to make the "cake"— a huge round tea biscuit cut horizontally and then cut into triangles like a pie. Mom made a mashed strawberry compote out of most of the berries and spooned it over the cake slices. Then the top slice was smothered in freshly whipped cream and decorated with whole berries. I can still taste the sweet strawberries in the cream.

My father loved this dessert. When Mom satisfied Dad's desire to have a traditional wife, doing wifely things, cooking what he liked, all was right with the world. This was one of those few times I felt glad to be in my family.

There was no end to summer jobs in the country and I was always eager to earn money. I spent part of several summers working for Mr. Seeley from Toronto who owned acres and acres of land about a mile north of our property. We called his property the tree plantation. He'd dug the huge pond that supplied irrigation water, and built a greenhouse where he grew evergreen seedlings to plant on the property. My job was to carefully remove a tiny seedling from each miniature pot in the greenhouse, dab the root with growth powder, and then replant it into a slightly bigger pot.

When I was back there alone with Mr. Seeley, especially when we stopped for lunch, I watched him carefully to make sure he wasn't hinting that he wanted to touch me. At least this time my parents' trust wasn't misplaced but, though he never did anything remotely like what the Teacher had done, I remained uneasy.

Other country jobs included picking raspberries, pruning Christmas trees, and, as I got older, pulling and bundling trees at the Orono forestry. For the boys, there was work on tobacco farms in the late summer to provide families with much-needed extra income.

* * *

The summer I was twelve, my family went on a camping trip to Midland, Ontario, and visited the Martyrs' Shrine Church. At this time, I was deeply devoted to the Catholic faith—I even contemplated becoming a nun. I was so enamoured with my faith, I did the outdoor Stations of the Cross at the Martyr's Shrine. I spent my hard-earned summer money on mass cards and a book that gave me fire and brimstone—gory details of the deaths of the Catholic martyrs at the hands of Indigenous people.

My parents also took us to a recreated Huron village that purportedly showed us the way early Huron people lived. We saw longhouses that seemed snug, meat and fish being dried, clothing made from deer skin.

But something that summer altered dramatically my vision of the Bible as a true and honest text. My parents had spent some time with a couple at the campground we were staying in, and I started to talk with the man about my religious beliefs. I'm not sure why my parents thought it was fine that their twelve-year-old daughter spent time alone with a strange man, but perhaps they knew he was a philosopher, not a molester. When I argued with him that the world was created in six days, just as the Bible said, he asked a very simple question that changed my thinking forever: "What if, way back then, days were a different length of time than they are today?"

That question turned my thinking on its head and allowed me to question things that, up to that point, I hadn't. On the way home from camping, I still read, with both fervour and disgust, those pamphlets that told what the martyrs had endured. I specifically remember the parts about Native people cutting off pieces of the priests' flesh and eating them—but doubt had entered my thoughts. What about the array of crutches in the Martyrs' Shrine church— were they really tossed aside when true believers were able to walk again, or simply placed there for the benefit of us, the tourists?

What was right, what was wrong? Had I been too rigid, too polarized in my thinking? Years later, in my twenties, I left the church for good, firm in the belief that I would *not* go to hell for skipping mass on Sundays. However, religion is emotional rather than logical, so many years later I had my children baptized—just in case.

Summer holidays were only respites, though. In September, we children went back to Leskard School and the Teacher. My feelings at that time of year were mixed. I loved the smell of new erasers, pencils, and notebooks, the new readers that held such wonderful stories, and the move to a new row of desks in the classroom that indicated I was in the next grade. But, though I had new supplies each year, I was stuck with the same old Teacher.

Chapter 18
Winter

Winter seemed harsher out in the country—much worse than I'd experienced in the suburbs. I was eight and a half when we first moved to Leskard, and I walked to school alone—but from age ten and a half, when my sister began grade one, she and I walked together.

Getting ready in the winter to walk to school was a major production. Before leaving the house in the morning, I had to clothe myself in either a dress or skirt and blouse, put on a woollen pullover or cardigan, and pull on trousers to go under my skirt—which I'd have to take off as soon as I arrived at school. My sister and I put on large extra socks (likely Dad's old ones) over our shoes, and then rubber boots, pulled tight by straps that snapped onto the sides of the boots. Lastly, we pulled on our coats and hats and put the hoods up. While my mother helped my sister, she would instruct me to pull my hat down over my forehead, and wind my scarf around my neck and head over the hood to make sure my mouth and nose were completely covered—with only a slit to see through. Lastly, I pulled on my mitts. Mom handed each of us our lunch pails. As I walked, I breathed through the wool over my face, so it became wet, cold, and covered with icicles.

After my sister started school, it was my responsibility to get us both to school and back home safely. In the winter, when I put my head down into the wind, I lost sight of her, but if I looked up to try to see where she was, tears flooded my eyes.

Much of our way to and from school was past open farm fields. There were five-foot snow fences to stop some of the snow from blowing onto the road, but no trees to help deflect the wind. If there had been freezing rain, we attached metal crampons to our boots so we could walk on the ice. Sometimes I fell through the top crust of the snow drifts up to my thighs and had to stop, sometimes crying with cold and exhaustion, before I could force myself to forge on, for my sake and my sister's.

When we walked to school, we were heading east, so the prevailing westerly winds gave us a little push as we walked. On the way home, we were facing west so we leaned into the gusting cold wind as we forced our boots through snow piled up on the road, plodding uphill—each step a major accomplishment. I carried a lunch pail in one hand and had one hand free to hold the bottom part of my coat if it blew open due to the wind.

* * *

The Teacher always arrived at school early so he could write the day's lessons on the blackboard. The first kids were in the school yard by then and, when it was very cold, he let them come in early. We children were all covered up, but I sensed the Teacher watching us take off all our clothes... layer by layer... when we came inside. Off came the boots, the extra socks and mitts all soaked with snow, the coat, the scarf, the hat, and the trousers. We loaded the heat register in the middle of the classroom floor with our mitts and socks. Boots lay on their sides with the hope that some heat would penetrate the damp interiors.

In the 1950s, there were no plastic bags to put inside our boots to keep our socks dry. If we were lucky, our thick extra socks would be dry at the end of the day, but too often they got re-soaked at recess and lunch hour. If things went well, the extra socks and insides of the boots were only damp, and could be warmed by our feet as we walked home.

Most winters, our road and driveway were snowed in from November to April—the snow in the roads so deep no snow plough could get through to our driveway. Dad had to walk to the village and back to bring groceries on our toboggan because Mom was home with my little brother.

* * *

But winter was not just to be endured. I learned to enjoy what I could. Around our house, the snow drifts were so deep and hardened by the wind that, on mild winter days, my sister and I dug down into the drifts to make forts that had snow benches and cubby holes in the sides. We sledded down the hill next to the house, and skated on the frozen pond in the field. Some things I just had to accept and make the best of, or I would have been unhappy all the time.

Chapter 19
Sandwich Spread And Poverty

Every day at noon, the Teacher sat at his desk at the front of the classroom, eating his lunch and watching us, ever vigilant. When I first started school in Leskard, the Junior teacher, Mr. Long, also ate his lunch at the Teacher's desk. Any students who couldn't, because of distance, go home for lunch, ate in our classroom.

When Miss Cobbledick started to teach the younger children, she refused to sit with the Teacher. She said she felt "uneasy" around him, preferring to eat with her students in the upstairs classroom. When we met again at the church gathering so many years later, she told me that the Teacher wanted her to teach his students health and science and to let him teach the younger children music. She refused, feeling she had enough work to do, and besides, she was fully qualified to teach music to her own students.

I lived too far from the school to go home for lunch, so I had to eat in front of the Teacher every lunch hour. Pausing in between each bite, he made personal comments to us: "Is that a new dress, Shirley?" "Did you just get your hair cut, Marilyn?" "You kids will have to get practicing if we want to win at the music festival this year."

I tried not to look at him because, if I did, he would grin at me, that smirk I still see in my dreams.

I sat at my desk, opened my lunch box, took out my sandwich, and folded back the waxed paper wrapping. I knew that day it was crabmeat and mayonnaise on whole wheat bread. Mom had probably bought the canned crabmeat for herself but ran out of things to make sandwiches with that morning, so my sister and I got the crabmeat. It was one of my favourites, along with roast chicken or left-over cooked ham ground up with mayonnaise and chopped pickle. Way up on the list from peanut butter, though peanut butter with jam was tolerable. We usually got that just before Dad's payday, when everything else ran out.

I glanced around to see what other children had brought in their lunches. Most had brown bags so I knew they didn't have a drink. I looked just as one boy named Michael was opening his sandwich. I knew he had sandwich spread on white bread. Other children had it, too—a green pickle and mayonnaise mixture that came out of a jar. I envied them for those sandwiches on peanut butter days, but not today.

"What have you got?" I asked.

"Sandwich spread," Michael answered with a broad smile, "again." Michael usually smiled.

"Going sledding today?"

"Yes, but only if someone has one of the big toboggans. The small sleds are too fast for me."

"Me, too."

"You know that big bump at the bottom of the hill? Yesterday I went flying over it and smashed onto the rink."

One of the big boys had poured a pail full of water down the hill and, after it froze, the sled track was slick with ice. Once my sled left the top of the hill, I barely touched the ground until I hit the rink at the bottom. So, forget the sled, but the lure of the toboggan was too much to refuse.

A year behind me in school, Michael was one of the small boys, with brown hair, slight and short. I knew he spent a lot of the recess and lunch time trying to stand up to the big boys. Even when the Teacher stood outside to smoke, he didn't intervene when the bullies tormented us. We had to fend for ourselves.

That night while we did the dishes, I asked my mother, "Can I take sandwich spread sandwiches for lunch?" I wanted brown sugar sandwiches too, but there was no point in mentioning those.

"Sandwich spread is for putting on meat sandwiches," she said.

None of the children had meat in their sandwich spread sandwiches.

"But kids take them for lunch—just sandwich spread on bread."

"Those children come from families that can't afford to give them anything else for lunch. It's cheap and has no food value. It's not worth buying."

I ate the same kind of lunch in Leskard school as I had in my former schools—but other children didn't have what I had—further proof that our family was different. Should I be more careful about telling others what I had in my lunch pail? Did it matter to the other children? I remembered how the children fell on the salmon sandwiches my Mother donated for school parties, so I guess they did see the difference. And so did my mother.

After Christmas one year I phoned Janie and Marilyn Gregory, excited to tell them about the gifts I'd received. My mother cautioned me to tell them only about one or two of my smallest presents. She knew the Gregory family had little money for Christmas and she didn't want me to embarrass them.

* * *

Though my mother was not imaginative about what she cooked, she paid a lot of attention to the healthiness of what she gave our family to eat—hot cream of wheat on cold mornings, lunches made up of a sandwich, cookies or a piece of cake, and fruit if she had any in the kitchen, always with a drink in my thermos.

When we ate supper at night my mother explained why she was careful not to give us anything fried. "When you fry meat, it forms charcoal and that causes cancer."

So, our hamburger meat patties were baked in the oven until they were as hard and dry as hockey pucks—barely edible even when I drowned them in ketchup.

On Fridays, Catholics couldn't eat meat, so we often had macaroni and cheese baked in the oven with stewed tomatoes, or smoked fish from Newfoundland. Mom made pretty much the same meals week after week—lots of boiled potatoes and canned vegetables. On school days, dessert was often instant pudding, made by me when I got home from school, or fruit cocktail from a can. More interesting food was for weekends. One of my favourites was stir-fried vegetables with chicken, on rice, after she learned to cook a few Chinese dishes—but we very rarely had that. Dad had requests like bread pudding that no one liked but him, and apple pie that everyone loved.

* * *

That day, as I sat eating my lunch in the classroom, I thought about the contrast between my crabmeat sandwich and the sandwich spread sandwiches of my classmates. I had no idea of the circumstances of other families that might not be able to give their children meat sandwiches. One woman I interviewed told me that on her farm, when times were tough, it wasn't unusual to have oatmeal for supper. You ate what you were given and were thankful for what you got.

When I went to school, I began to look more closely at the other children. I knew many boys wore the same shirts most days but I hadn't really given it much thought until then. Was that because they were poor? What about the girls? One girl, Nancy, wore dresses that seemed too big for her. Her hair hung down close to the sides of her face so you could hardly see what she looked like, and her voice was very quiet.

One boy, Brian, was always smiling and laughing. Many years later when I interviewed Brian, I found out much more about his home life.

He talked about his older brother Dennis who was in high school. "He wants to get the highest marks he can so he can go to a university far away from here. I don't want him to—I'm afraid he'll never come back."

"Why wouldn't he come back?"

"Because of my dad and my brother Bob. They're always yelling. Dad yells at us and our mom. Sometimes he says things that don't make any sense."

His father was a World War two veteran. He was there on D-Day. Sometimes when Brian looked at him sleeping, he said he could see his father tense up as though he was being shot at—nightmares of wartime fighting. Twenty-eight men in his unit died on the beach. He never talked about what he had to do to stay alive. Brian had a certain admiration for what his father went through. "I never had a life like that. So, watching him sleep was my insight into what war was like."

Brian also had fond memories of my dad—said they went out hunting, and "talked beagles." My father was just young enough that, though he was called up during the war and trained at Trenton airfield, he never went overseas. His demons weren't the same as those that haunted Brian's father. In elementary school, it never occurred to me to say anything about my dad going to bed early on Saturday nights after drinking beer all afternoon. Or about how he pounded on the floor above the living room to keep us quiet.

Brian said that, even though his father and brother got way too angry about things, sometimes that came in handy. His brother had an argument with Mr. Bernston from the farm east of the village. Bernston owed his brother twenty dollars for helping with the haying. so when Bernston went to tend the cattle north on Brian's family's laneway, Bob put the hay fork to his throat and told him to pay up or else.

I'd never heard this story when we were young. "What happened?"

"He paid."

Brian's father and older brother hunted and fished so the family could eat. Brian had eaten porcupine, muskrat, snake and groundhog. I wasn't sure how porcupine or muskrat would be cooked, or how they would taste, but maybe they would be okay. Better than going hungry. Brian learned to hunt from an early age, but it is something that, now he is over seventy, he does reluctantly. He told me about sparing a doe that had three fawns with her.

My dad hunted and fished, too—game birds that Mom made into game pie. Under the crust, pieces of pheasant and partridge, sometimes rabbit, floated with potatoes, carrots, and celery in gravy. She also made trout and whitefish fried in butter. Dad shot groundhogs in the field next to our house and cooked them in big pots in the kitchen to feed his hunting dogs—not the family. The horrible smell always kept me out of the kitchen.

Brian told me about the time the Teacher had called out to him as he started out the classroom door at lunch hour to go into the boys' cloakroom.

The Teacher snickered as he asked, "Hey, did you finish your arithmetic this morning?"

"Not all of it," said Brian.

Brian was sometimes slow doing his school work.

"You should stay at your desk until you finish it."

"But I'll miss my lunch hour."

"Well then, you'll stay after school to finish it. It's up to you."

Brian had to get home right after school to help with chores. He sighed and went back into the classroom.

As the Teacher ate his cookies, he looked at Brian and, in a semi-whispering sneer, said, "You'll never amount to anything." The Teacher wiped the crumbs off his face with his serviette and put away his lunch pail.

Chapter 20
The Teacher Is Here To Stay

I don't know when I understood I was in Leskard School... with the Teacher... to stay. The village and the school board had spoken and my parents fell in line with the decision to ignore the complaints against the Teacher. Were they just apathetic, or were they complicit in some way like the rest of the villagers? Was it all too much for villagers to admit what was going on and then do something? Did they not want to do anything that would upset the life of the village—or their own lives? Was it too onerous a task to listen to the children and fire the Teacher? Was it easier to do nothing?

No one was going to alter the fact that I had a molester as a teacher—unless our family moved out of the village. My parents did put our house up for sale at some point but I don't remember when. In my memory, it seems it was for sale because living in the country was too hard, dealing with snow, a lack of water, no modern conveniences, miles from nowhere. Nothing to do with the Teacher, but I don't know. The house didn't sell, so they took it off the market.

I never consciously sat down and said to myself, well this is how it is. Though I must have had high hopes initially when the Teacher was revealed for who he was, because I wrote in my diary on January 15, 1959, "He needs to be put out of the school." At ten years old, I realized we had a monster in our midst and what should be done, but I had no power, no say in what happened. The village talked about the Teacher and then it didn't. As time went by, for the most part, I was only aware of my discomfort. Now I know I was in a form of denial—the whole thing slipped from my conscious life only to come out years later in the form of dreams, anxiety, depression, and my reaction to a colleague when I was in Prague.

* * *

Who was this man—Mr. Pollard, the Teacher, the Principal? In order to paint a picture of him, I have to draw on my own memories and impressions from the five years he was my teacher, and combine that with information from my classmates like Jill and Cathy, villagers Joan Gimblett and Ken Frame who had been in school with him, and others, like Joan Ransberry who lived in the area and added more details, until a consistent picture emerged.

The Teacher wasn't always The Teacher. He was born in 1930 to Laura and George Pollard who lived on the ninth concession of Clarke Township, just north of Leskard. The Pollards had a girl first, who died when only a month old, and then Jim, the boy who would later become the Teacher. The men in the family were active in the community. They were members of the Kirby church, and large landowners. In the Orono Times and the book *Picture the Way We Were: Darlington and Clarke,* there is a picture of Jim Pollard when he was an adolescent playing in the Orono Band.

In one interview, the Teacher's father, George, was described as looking "bright-eyed, sort of gnomish," and very "sharp in the money sense." He would go alone to the Leskard village store to do the grocery shopping—not accompanied by Laura, the Teacher's mother. She rarely socialized, was rarely seen, and was said to be under George's thumb. Did she suffer from depression or agoraphobia? Prolonged grief over the loss of her first baby?

We will never know now. When the Pollards moved to Orono, she would often bake treats and serve them to children in the neighbourhood.

The Pollards were one of "the old, established, and rather pompous families," "well respected," "an elite family, long in the area, and involved in the church and the community," according to Joan, who grew up on her family farm northeast of Leskard and had attended Enterprise School. She heard stories about Jim Pollard when she was young and remembered an "emotional discussion" between her parents—they had heard the rumours, too. She said that when the Pollard issue came up, her father said it was up to the people in Leskard to deal with the situation.

In the fifties and sixties, there was "such a pecking order and such restrictions during those times... many people were so shy, so private, and so suspicious." Joan considered it a non-supportive society, in which denial was a way of life. There were "unwritten rules" that indicated to all what was to be talked about and what not to say. She also said that "some of the families in rural areas were 'without eyes.' They either didn't see or minimized serious issues." In other words, if they don't allow ourselves to really see and acknowledge what is going on, they won't see anything wrong.

* * *

I interviewed Joan Lewis in her home just south of Calgary. She had been born into a family of twelve children, grew up in the village—and was a wealth of information. Her time as a pupil in Leskard School overlapped with the Teacher's when he was a child. She described "Little Jimmy" as always weird—somewhat aggressive, a bit less normal. She said the girls didn't want him to touch them with his soft, fat, pudgy fingers—so he obviously tried, even at that young age. The boys didn't want to hang around with him either, because he was "different."

His parents gave him "whatever he wanted." He was a spoiled bully who grew into a large fleshy boy/man who used to buy booze for the teens in the village because he was older than they were.

Joan told a similar story to others in the village—after the complaints were made about the Teacher, many villagers simply didn't believe it.

* * *

Ken Frame came to the event at the church in 2018 where I first announced my project. The following summer, 2019, when I returned to Ontario to do more research, I drove into his driveway across from the old Leskard school. He came out of his house and when I stepped out of my car, he said, "You're the Lee girl." He invited me to sit on his porch where he freely told me about the Teacher.

Ken was born the same year as Jim Pollard. He had not only known Pollard, they had been in the same class in Leskard school. He told me that, as a young child, the Teacher had a head of bushy black hair, but by the time he had reached his twenties and started teaching, he was prematurely bald. Pollard started his primary school years as a pupil in Leskard (where he was taught for one year by Jill's mother). He also spent a couple of years at Oak School, another country school a few miles east on concession road eight, where his mother's family had a farm. Then he returned to Leskard to finish grade eight. Ken and Jim went to high school at the same time. Ken wasn't a good student, but Jim was "good in music, smart at school."

Jimmy got up to mischief. He stole batteries out of cars just for the heck of it, and threw them in the creek—he didn't sell them, he didn't need the money. His parents gave him anything he wanted, and his uncle in Bowmanville regularly gave him money. He wanted for nothing. As an adult, he hung around former students of his: Ricky Anderson, who had been in my grade, and Ronnie Ball. They used to go to dances together to pick up women. He acknowledged the damage done to young girls by the Teacher with his comment to me, "It still bothers you after all these years," which I confirmed.

* * *

During the two interviews I had with Jill, she told me many things about herself, her family, and their relationship to the Teacher. Jill's father's brother had married the Teacher's aunt, making them relatives, extended family. She told her aunt about the Teacher and was greeted with a scolding.

Jill had visited the Teacher's house a few times, and couldn't resist peeking into his bedroom when she went upstairs to use the washroom.

She said that when the Teacher was young, his mother had decorated his bedroom, and it had stayed the same, even as the Teacher grew older—decorated to suit children of the age he liked—eight to ten-year-olds—a shrine to childhood.

Jill wondered if the Teacher's parents hadn't allowed him to grow up, but I think it was more complex than that. The Teacher may still have had one foot in childhood, but he had the power of an adult—and he used that power.

* * *

Given his tendencies, it was much better for the Teacher to apply to teach at the small country school in Leskard rather than schools in the larger towns. There, he would just be a regular teacher, always under the watchful eye of the Principal and Vice Principal. In Leskard, with his father on the local school board, he got to *be* the Principal, ruler of his own domain, the top guy, the boss, in his navy suit and tie.

When people started gossiping about the Teacher at the general store, he must have been pretty nervous. Soon girls were kept home from school, like Cathy, my sister, the Anderson girl, and me. When the inspector came to talk with him, he must have thought he was "in for it," but from what Mom told me, he just kept telling people that the girls misunderstood him when he helped them with their school work or with getting their coats on. I'd told my mother the Teacher pushed back my skirt in order to see my new crinoline, which he complimented, but he told the school inspector he was only crouching down to check my arithmetic and my skirt was folded back. He couldn't help seeing it. He said I *had* missed the nurse's visit. Maybe he explained that he had to take me upstairs during recess to ask the same questions the nurse would have asked—and touch me in the way the nurse would have. He protested that I had misunderstood the whole thing—like Cathy had. It was all our fault.

His father must have been angry when the news about his son became public. I can imagine George Pollard, his face beet red, his mouth wide open, shouting at his son, "What the hell were you doing? DID you put your hands on these girls? Put your hand up their dresses? That's what they're saying at the store. Your mother and I are totally embarrassed—what were you thinking? Keep quiet and we'll deny everything. Just keep your hands to yourself from now on."

But possibly his father was trying to cover his own sins. Ken Frame had said to me, "Like father, like son." There was a restaurant George Pollard couldn't go into anymore. The waitresses told the owner he grabbed them, tried to kiss them, and came behind the counter to do it. When Ken had George over to help with a window installation, he was afraid to have his young wife around.

Now I realize the Teacher likely couldn't help how he felt about little girls. In his mind, there we were, every day at school, flouncing our skirts in front of him, skipping rope so our skirts blew up exposing our legs, wearing short socks and strappy shoes. But watching wasn't enough for him—he needed to touch us. Treatment might have helped him if it had been available in the fifties and sixties, but it wasn't—not until the late seventies. And he would either have to admit what he was doing in order to seek out therapy, or he would have to be convicted of a crime.

Abusive people are not just abusive—they can do good things too—that's what makes it all so complex and confusing—and, for children, difficult to figure out. When I grew up and married, my first husband was abusive, but he could also be charming. That theme has followed me in my life—the notion that if only someone were all bad, it would be so much easier to detect—and no one is all bad.

The Teacher must have done some inner bargaining because he never touched me in exactly the same way again after my sister and I returned to school. But there were lots of other girls in the village whose parents hadn't made a fuss, who didn't want to get involved—like Jill, whose mother and father were related to the Teacher. He was likely confident they wouldn't cause a problem. And the Spry family was gone, moved away, so no longer a problem.

Chapter 21
The Teacher's Obsession

Some parents in the village hid their heads in the sand—as one man I interviewed said about his family—sacrificing their dignity and sometimes their children in order to maintain the fantasy that nothing was happening in Leskard School. One such family was the Gregorys.

Mrs. Gregory was a widow. Her son was already married and living some distance away, but her two younger daughters attended Leskard school. She said nothing when the Teacher began to pay an excessive amount of attention to Marilyn.

Janie and Marilyn Gregory both had good voices—and music was the Teacher's passion. He taught us key signatures, notes, and scales—telling us that, by the time we were in grade eight, we had learned the equivalent of grade two music theory.

Through my interviewing, I realized that most of the children knew Marilyn Gregory was the Teacher's favourite. When she stood up to go out to recess or to the washroom, he watched her. Sometimes when he called her up to his front desk to check her school work, he turned his knees to the side so she could sit on his lap. But he did this with many girls, so we were used to it.

The girls the Teacher usually showed an interest in were between the ages of eight and ten—but even as Marilyn grew older, she remained his focus. She wasn't tall and she was very slight like a younger girl, with curly red hair, and a singing voice that could win prizes at the local music festival.

She became his, the predator's, "chosen child, special and desirable." (Kristjanson 2013)

Every year the Teacher prepared some of our class to compete in the music festival. Nine girls, including me, were chosen to compete in the triple trio, and Janie and Marilyn, Leslie Anderson, and I practiced to compete in the duets. Marilyn also competed in the solo category. The Teacher had to coach her of course and, since she'd be doing a solo, he had to spend a lot of time with her—alone. In addition, because he'd entered her and her sister Janie into the duet category, he spent even more time with her.

On the day of the duet competition at the festival, there were only four of us competing, so the Teacher drove us, all squashed into his black VW bug. The Teacher was proud of his Volkswagen beetle with the engine in the back—the section normally reserved for the trunk of a car. He may have had the only one in Clarke township. Most people drove cars or trucks manufactured in Oshawa at General Motors because that was the big employer in the area.

After our family bought a Chevrolet Corvair, a car that also had its engine in the rear, the Teacher took me aside at noon. "How does your family like your new car?" He commented on how wonderful the engine in the rear was. How it made so much sense—especially in the winter when you need more weight on the back tires to drive in the snow.

What did I know about cars? I may have been eleven or twelve at the time, I can't remember, but I do remember feeling awkward. Why was the Teacher talking to me about such things? My father made those decisions. But I confess, I was also flattered that a grown up thought me knowledgeable. And proud that our family had a new, modern car. I had no idea at the time that engaging children in grown-up talks was something men did who shared the Teacher's predilections.

When the date arrived for the triple trio chorus to compete, there were nine girls to transport. The Teacher brought another man along—a stranger—to drive some of us. I can't remember what his name was or how the Teacher introduced him to us. Were they friends? Did this other man also want to put himself in the midst of children, by accompanying us? I couldn't trust the Teacher to bring along a safe person.

On the way to the competition, we stopped at a restaurant for lunch. It was a Friday, the day Catholics are forbidden to eat meat, but I forgot and ordered a ham sandwich. The strange man snickered at me, looked at the Teacher and said, "Looks like she's in the wrong pew." *The man knew I was Catholic*—the Teacher must have told him. He had discussed me with this suspicious stranger.

As my face grew hot under his stare, I called the waitress over, "Can I please change my order to an egg salad sandwich?" While I'd rescued myself from sin, I've never forgotten how embarrassed and ashamed I felt when my mistake was laid open for all to see—and comment on.

Our triple trio won the competition and we were invited to appear on television in Peterborough. My parents let me go, with the Teacher, this time at night for this performance. Nothing was said about keeping safe, or keeping my distance from the Teacher. My mother only lamented that the TV reception was so bad that night she couldn't see me on television.

* * *

My mom liked Mrs. Gregory, and stopped by her house for a cup of tea and gossip now and again. Mom had started to sell Avon, so possibly Mrs. Gregory bought Avon products from her. Avon and a visit gave Mom lots of information.

As the Teacher's fixation on Marilyn grew, so did his desire to see her more often, even during weekends and holiday periods. My mother heard the story from her mother and the village buzzed with the news.

Mrs. Gregory and her girls would drive into their driveway and see the Teacher's car parked—sometimes near their driveway, sometimes across the dirt road. The Teacher would look, sometimes smile—perhaps he was trying to see if Marilyn was in the car.

My mother asked Marilyn's mother, "Have you said anything to him? Warned him off?"

"No, we don't want to cause any trouble." Like my mother, she talked with the neighbours, but didn't deal directly with the problem of the Teacher. And, as so many other families did, Marilyn's mother did nothing as she watched her young, attractive daughters leave the house each morning to walk to school.

Two people I interviewed said the Gregory girls received favours from the Teacher. One man said they "took advantage of Jim," implying that they had the power. However, the girls were children and Pollard an adult. As youngsters in a family that had a hard time making ends meet, possibly the extra attention was welcome. Who could blame them for wanting to be special? But possibly they just didn't know what to do.

For most families, problems with the Teacher had been happening out of their sight, behind the school walls, but now the Teacher was coming to a student's driveway. He wasn't contained within the school—he could come to our homes. Also, undoubtedly, the Teacher fantasized about us, the girls in our school. He plotted and planned what he would say and do, even before he put his hands on our legs. He had planned to sit at the end of the Gregorys' driveway.

When I was young, I didn't know the name for what the Teacher was doing, but I do now—stalking. He was stalking an eleven-year-old girl.

My mother questioned Marilyn's mother about what she was going to do about the attention her daughter was getting from the Teacher. Mom told me Mrs. Gregory's plan. She would send Marilyn away for the summer to stay at her older brother's home.

After my mother told me this, I wasn't sure that would really solve the problem of the Teacher's obsession. I knew he wouldn't give up. Yes, Marilyn would be away for two months—but were they going to tell him she'd left the village for the summer? Plus, she'd be back at the end of August to return to school. And why did *she* have to go away? No one had told the Teacher to go anywhere.

Later, Mom confirmed my fear—sending Marilyn to her brother's hadn't solved the problem. The Teacher was spotted parked on his road—over one hundred miles from our village.

When I was a child, I just reacted with fear to this information about the lengths the Teacher would go to see Marilyn. I couldn't do anything about it. I had to shove it away with everything else I was forced to ignore. But now, as an adult, I feel outrage. Questions go through my head. How had he found out where she had gone? How did he know where her older brother lived? What was he doing there? What did he hope would happen? Was he at all aware of how inappropriate this was?

In addition, why did my mother tell me all this? What sense could I make of her constantly reporting to me the Teacher's actions? Did she do it because she disapproved of him? Rather than taking action herself, was she warning me about him, though indirectly, so *I* would take action? What could *I* do?

I suspect now she was just using me as a gossip companion, unaware of what that did to me. It certainly didn't make anything better—in fact, knowing that she knew about his actions, and disapproved, but still sent us to school, made things worse. She wasn't ignorant of his ongoing behaviour. She just wasn't doing anything about it.

Chapter 22
Some Fathers Did Something - Where Was Mine?

As I thought back to those days in Leskard school, I realized that most of the conversation between my parents and me went through my mother. Where was my father in all those concerns about the Teacher? Why didn't he do what Mr. Tyler did?

After Margie Tyler left the class when she'd yelled at the Teacher, Mr. Tyler, her father, came to the school. Knocked on the door. Though I might have been there when this all happened, I can only report on the incident from what others have told me—either I don't remember it, or it might have happened when my sister and I were kept home after Cathy Spry's story came out. Also, there were two versions to this story. In one, Mr. Tyler had a gun, in the other, he didn't.

When the Teacher answered the door, Mr. Tyler showed him his shotgun or his fist and, by all reports, told him to "Get outside here. I'm going to beat the livin' daylights out of you."

The Teacher stood in the front door of the school. The men who remembered this incident said they could hear Mr. Tyler say, "If you ever touch my daughter again, this is what will be waiting for you." Then he either waved the gun or his fist around.

The Teacher stepped backwards into the school. "Okay, Al, no need for any of that. No one is touching your daughter or anyone else's. There's nothing like that happening."

According to those who told the story, Mr. Tyler didn't believe him, but couldn't do much other than threaten him. He turned to leave and told him one more time so the Teacher would get the message that, yes, he would leave, but he should mind what he was saying. "Don't you touch Margie again."

Did *my* father care that his daughter had been molested, that other girls were being molested? I wondered if he had gone to the school and threatened the Teacher like Mrs. Spry or Mr. Tyler had done, and I just hadn't been told. Or was he too nervous? Too afraid to touch matters that had to do with sexuality? If he thought my mother was the best one to look after all that sort of thing, he was wrong.

* * *

Dad had other things to occupy his attention. He loved to walk in the forest, miles north of our home. He wild crafted, which meant he brought home native plants for us to eat. He had regular routes where he knew there were fiddleheads in the spring, and puffballs in late summer. Sliced puffball fried in butter was one of my favourites, as well as fiddleheads steamed and served with butter and salt. One time he came home very excited. He had found a large morel mushroom patch, collected them, and brought them home. Mom sliced them, fried them in butter, and served them for supper—so delicious—though when I got sick, I discovered I was horribly allergic to them.

My dad loved to hunt and fish and had done so, even when he was in high school. In fact, he met his best friend at the Oshawa Skeet and Gun Club—the man we children called Uncle Bill.

One time, Dad and his hunting pals took a trailer to sleep in when they went deer hunting. From that time on, Dad told me the story about how smoking saved his life. He woke up in the middle of the night in the trailer. As he usually did, he took out his cigarettes to have a smoke before going back to sleep. He tried several times to light the match—with no success. He was puzzled, and decided to go outside to light up. As soon as he opened the trailer door, a rush of air hit him. When he stepped out, he lit his match and figured out what had happened. Because of the cool evening, they'd lit a gas heater in the trailer. It had used up all the oxygen. Indeed, if Dad hadn't been addicted to his smokes, he and all the hunters could have died.

I knew how much my father loved Belle, his best bird dog. He had her bred to several champion Brittany spaniels over the years. But dogs come into heat or fertility every six months so, at those times, females had to be controlled, penned up, guarded—protected. We had to make sure Belle didn't get outside, escape while in heat. But one time she did, and ran into the field to the east of our house, where a male dog mounted her as soon as she reached him. My father yelled and screamed, blue with anger.

Nine weeks later Belle's puppies were born. Instead of the beautiful orange and white of purebred Brittany spaniels, they were black. My father took them from her, put them into a bag, and attached the bag to the exhaust pipe at the back of our car until they stopped squealing. Then he buried the bag in the field. It sickened him, and he swore never to do this again—get rid of animals that he deemed not worthy of life.

Dad hunted game birds and deer in the autumn when it was hunting season, rabbits when he could. When he brought partridge, pheasant, grouse, and ducks home after a day's hunting, he took out most of the feathers outdoors, before bringing them into the house. He spread newspapers on top of the dining table, laid down the blue-skinned bird bodies, and cut them open.

From the time we moved to the country, he showed me the different parts of the birds' insides. Nothing was as fascinating to him as the gizzard. It contained tiny stones that would grind up the food—berries and grain—everything the bird had recently eaten. I could see all the parts of the digestive system laid out on the newspaper. He pulled out the ends of the feathers, and the shot—the tiny round pellets that had killed the birds. Sometimes he didn't get them all and our teeth crunched on them when we ate the roasted meat.

While Dad cleaned the birds, he often asked me to get him a beer, "Bring the bottle here and I'll show you how to pour it."

I ran into the kitchen, thrilled to be asked to help him—I loved my dad. Mom handed me a beer glass from the cupboard. I got a bottle out of the fridge, the opener from the cutlery drawer, and carried them all into the room we called the "big kitchen" where we ate. I placed them on the table, being careful not to get them too close to the pheasant or quail guts.

Dad picked up the bottle and opener, popped the top, and then said, "Hold it like this." He demonstrated with the bottle, holding the glass on an angle. "When you pour the beer slowly like this, it doesn't make a head." The foam on the top of the beer. "See, that's how you do it. Now, you try."

I took the bottle and glass from him and imitated his pouring action.

"Good," he said and smiled at me.

I'd pleased my father. I never did skin a pheasant but I was proud that, as a young child, I knew the proper way to pour beer. I put the bottle down and handed him the full glass.

Hunting and drinking beer went together for my father, hand in glove. All his hunting buddies drank—and drank lots. It was part of his life as a man, and in particular, an outdoorsman. When he went deer hunting, case after case of beer went into the back of the station wagon. Unfortunately, his drinking wasn't limited to hunting trips.

Every Sunday morning, Mom, my brother, sister, and I got ready for church. As I write this, I'm looking at a photo taken when I was twelve, standing beside my mother and looking down at my brother and sister. I'm slouching a bit because, by that time, I was taller than my mother—and she was the boss. She's looking straight at the camera while my eyes are partially hidden by the light blue cat's-eye style prescription glasses I'd worn from the time I was in grade five. My dark curly hair hangs down on either side of my face. An awkward-looking hat sits on my head. We are heading out to church. Dad snapped the photo, so he was out of bed, but after taking the picture, he waved us goodbye and headed back into the house as we drove down the driveway. There is no joy on my face, no smile for the camera.

Dad usually stayed in bed on a Sunday morning, even though it was he who was Catholic originally—Mom had converted in order to marry him. When we got home from church, Dad would be sitting in his favourite chair with a large glass of tomato juice and Worcestershire sauce—his hangover remedy. It must have worked because he used it for years—all the time I lived at home. Sometimes he looked pretty rough as he drank his remedy, but by Monday, he was sober and could go to work. He didn't have to stay sober for us, his family, but he did have to for work.

* * *

I knew Dad was proud of my interest in school work and the high marks I got on exams. I knew, though he never actually told me directly. When I got my report card, I would bring it home, show it to my mother and, if Dad was home, he would look it over and say, "Only 98%? What happened to the other two percent—did you spell your name wrong?" He'd laugh. I was then to smile, blush, turn away. That was our routine.

If Dad was on night shift, the report card was left on the kitchen table. Dad would look at it when he got home at three in the morning from the motors. When I got up in the morning for school, there would be a note telling me how pleased he was about my results—signed "Your loving Dad." So, I knew—he was proud of me and loved me—at arm's length.

But the big issue remained—with all that love, they had allowed a pedophile to teach their children.

Chapter 23
Growing Up Under The Gaze Of The Teacher

Two months past my eleventh birthday, in the midst of grade six, I noticed blood on my panties. I knew what it was. A few months earlier, Mom had sat me down in the living room and placed a thick book with a green cover on my lap—*The Family Health Encyclopedia*. According to my mother, it would tell me everything I needed to know about getting older. She went into the kitchen to prepare supper.

The book was open to a page that had line drawings of a woman with her insides pictured. Nothing much that looked like my body. The pages explained monthly cycles, hormones, ovaries, and the uterus, but I had no idea what any of it meant. I sat on the couch reading.

When I finished, Mom came back from the kitchen and said, "When you see blood on your underwear, tell me. I have supplies for you."

So, when I saw the blood, I went to her. My mother got out a box of sanitary pads and a white elastic belt she had in preparation for my first period. She got a pad out of the box and handed it to me. She showed me how to attach it so it would stay in place, how to remove the stained pad, and dispose of it so our dogs wouldn't get into it. "Wrap it tightly in two paper bags and then put it into the bathroom waste basket."

This was a new period of my life, no pun intended. Barely eleven and now with the body of a young woman, I was already taller than most of the children in the school. I was a bit unsure about it all, but generally, I accepted this "new me"—until I realized that my period would last for several days and I'd have to change pads while at school. How was I going to do that?

Mom suggested I take a small purse to school with an extra pad so I could change it in the washroom.

In grade six, I never usually took a purse to school and was afraid someone would ask about it. But my biggest concern was, I'd have to put my hand up to ask to go to the washroom. What if the Teacher noticed me taking a purse with me? Would he know what was in it? What it was for? If so, then he would know this personal thing about me. About my body, my underwear, my periods. The Teacher knew us, the girls in his class, knew our bodies. He watched us. He touched us. He knew whether I usually carried a purse. All these thoughts went through my head when I asked to go to the washroom the next day.

We girls didn't talk among ourselves about having periods and I didn't talk about it at home unless I had to. Mom had a code word for the pads— "blades"—so the real word would never appear on the grocery list. It wasn't until I was an adult that it hit me—the word my mother used for sanitary pads was an instrument that could draw blood. All those years ago, it was just the word I had to use.

Usually my mother did the shopping, but in the winter when we were snowed in, it fell to my father to bring home things we'd run out of—including my pads. We had a system. Either I'd tell Mom I'd run out or I'd put it on the shopping list using the code word. Then she would give the list to Dad. When he got home, he'd hand the brown paper bag containing the Kotex box to Mom and she'd hand it to me. I'd quickly take the paper bag and hide it in the back of the cupboard under the large sink in the bathroom. The whole business wasn't just private—it was shameful—and had to remain hidden.

I remember days when I was angry—no, furious—that I was a girl. There seemed to be so many problems because I was female—the Teacher only molested girls, my mother was afraid of me doing things she considered wrong, the supplies for my period had to be hidden, girls could get into "trouble." No one said anything about boys getting into trouble.

At age eleven and for many years after, I had no idea what the relationship was between having a period and sexuality. I didn't know what sex was or how babies came to be. Because of my mother's hysterectomy, I had never seen her pregnant and she never had periods. But I did realize that some things were just not talked about—or they were talked about in a certain "taboo" way.

My mother heard about an unmarried girl in the village who was in "trouble"—pregnant at seventeen years of age. She didn't explain how that had happened, but as I grew older I figured out it had something to do with cars—what, I wasn't sure. If a girl got into a car with a boy something must happen that resulted in pregnancy. I thought that was why my mother wouldn't let me date or ride in a car with a boy until I was nearly seventeen. And even then, only to go to the formal dance at the high school.

As I grew into adolescence, I learned about relationships, sex, and love in disjointed bits and pieces. I knew that what the Teacher had done to me was wrong, but not that it had anything to do with sex. I knew the village girl getting pregnant was wrong but had no idea of the mechanics—perhaps she *had* been in a car with a boy. I knew that masturbating was "impure" in the eyes of the Catholic church, but not that it had anything to do with sex, or was connected in any way to what the Teacher had done.

My Mother absolutely forbade Sandra Dee or Annette Funicello movies, and I knew that Elvis Presley movies were too "racy" for me, but not why. I could watch movies at the Regent Theatre in Oshawa, but not at the Marks Theatre— my mother implied that the Marks wasn't good. Did they show those racy teen movies there? When a grown man looked at me in a bathing suit, standing on the side of a swimming pool, and said that I looked beautiful and desirable, when I was only twelve, I knew it was wrong because of how uncomfortable it made me feel.

I was surrounded by circumstances in which distorted sexual desire dominated. At school, the Teacher had the power. At home, Mother and Dad made punitive rules rather than providing guidance. Where was I to learn about my own life, love, romance, and sex?

* * *

When I was about twelve, the man we children called Uncle Bill, my Dad's best friend, and hunting, fishing, drinking buddy since they were sixteen, visited Mom while Dad was at work. When Dad found out, he blew up.

"He *knew* I was working days! *What* was he doing here?"

"He's having problems with his marriage. You know what Evelyn is like. He needed someone to talk to."

I never knew if that was fast thinking on Mom's part, or the truth. If I'd been at home when he visited, I might have felt the same uncomfortableness I'd experienced years before when the next door neighbour's son used to visit. But I wasn't. Back then, I had no reason to suspect anything was wrong.

After a strained couple of months, Dad and Uncle Bill went back to hunting, fishing, and drinking.

* * *

Mom decided I was old enough to be fitted for my first bra when I was twelve, nearly thirteen. We went to Eaton's, the largest store in the nearest big town, Oshawa, to visit their women's underwear department. In the early sixties, men knew enough not to wander into that section of the store, and movies featured comic scenes of men turning red with embarrassment if they took a wrong turn into "Women's Lingerie."

The sales lady measured me and tut-tutted about my size. My mother had waited until my breasts had developed beyond the training bra stage. That meant nothing to me at the time, but I guess they were too big to be trained. I didn't have a choice of style—Mom purchased a plain white cotton bra for me.

Back home, no one told me how to adjust the straps, so my breasts hung too low as I struggled to keep them inside "the cups"—creating a questionable profile under sweaters.

Also, I was never told what breasts were for, so when someone on television said something about breastfeeding, I looked at my mother in surprise.

She turned to me and raised her voice, "What did you *think* they were for? Filling out sweaters?"

I burned with shame. I had no idea what my breasts were for. I thought they just developed because I was a girl. I didn't know. But I knew enough not to reply. I had inadvertently said something wrong, taboo even. Like my periods, feeding babies was something that had to be hidden, something to be ashamed of.

"Big for my age." That's what they called it. As though I had an affliction. Five foot nine and only twelve, I exceeded the expected size of a typical twelve-year-old. That year my mother sewed the slim skirt I craved after seeing pictures of Betty and Veronica in the Archie comics. After I wore it once, it disappeared. Mom said she didn't know where it went. Perhaps her hope was that, in a full skirt, I would look less like a woman so my Teacher wouldn't look at me. But my mother got it all backwards.

"He should have been married," she said. "That would solve his problem."

My mother looked for easy answers to life's issues. How could I explain to her that his preferred bride would be nine or ten years old? I barely understood myself that he wasn't interested in women. He liked little girls.

* * *

In the winter, we couldn't go outside to play baseball or practice for field day for physical education. Instead, on Friday afternoons, the Teacher told us to push our desks to the sides of the classroom. He brought in records to play and his own record player. He lined us up in pairs down the centre of the room, boys and girls opposite each other, and taught us to dance.

I liked dancing—the music, the rhythm, the orderliness, and predictability of the steps. We learned the waltz and foxtrot first. The Teacher said they were the easiest to learn. One two three four, one two three four, make a box on the floor as we stepped to the music. Once we mastered this, we learned more complicated dance steps, like the tango and rhumba. I suspect he learned to dance at the Arthur Murray Studios in Oshawa, the mecca for single unattractive men, but we were a group of nine- to fourteen-year-old children moving our hips to Latin American rhythms. The Teacher demonstrated the steps—using all us girls as partners.

One January day, the Teacher motioned for me to come into the centre of the classroom "dance floor." He pressed his fingers sharply into my back as he guided me through the steps. When he pulled me to his chest, I had to place my left hand on the rough woollen shoulder of his blue suit. He held my slim young hand in his oversized fingers. His neck bulged, squeezed out above the stiff collar of his shirt. His round face leered at me, caught there in the middle of a twirl. My stomach clenched. I turned my face to the side so I couldn't smell his breath. Relieved when he let me dance with the boys in my class, I could breathe again.

Mom kept getting it wrong. She'd told me never to be in a room alone with the Teacher, but not how to manage that. I never knew what to say to him when he wanted to talk with me alone—and my mother didn't seem to realize that his obsessions and behaviour didn't stop—ever. Some of his inappropriate actions were out in the open for all of us to see. The hand that circled our waists in the dance lessons was the same hand that had gone up our legs. We couldn't escape the violating fingers, even in front of a room full of other children. And, even if *I* could have escaped, was it all right with her if he did it to others?

The Teacher was an intruder on our innocence—like a bug that crawls up inside your shorts. We were a group of girls tightly bound by the Teacher's invasion of our bodies.

In order to cope with an adult man who had insinuated his way into my childhood, and with adults around me denying what was going on, I had to shut down. I had to disavow my right to respect, to privacy, to my own body, and, like the adults in the village, act as though everything was normal. I had to fake it if I were to survive, but it was all so unconscious—so natural, I didn't know I was doing it. When the Teacher began to appear in my dreams after I married at age twenty-one, I knew the bug had crept even inside the depths of my mind.

* * *

Like all young girls, I fantasized about boys, dances, going on dates, falling in love. I bought a "love comic" at the corner General Store that my mother threw into the garbage as soon as I brought it home. I wanted to be Annette Funicello, but instead of "Tall Paul," my romance would be with a classmate. I had a crush on a new boy every few weeks or so, and wrote in my diary about any new fantasy boyfriend.

Boys were all in my imagination until I visited my old best friend and neighbour, Janie, who still lived in Courtice, where we used to live. She took me to a beach party where we ate hot dogs, drank pop, danced to popular music, and met boys. One in particular was named Doug. I wrote in my diary about this "divine, polite, charming boy" with blond, curly hair and blue eyes. I was completely infatuated—normal at age twelve. He was fourteen and in grade nine.

Several months later when I visited Janie again, he came over to visit because he knew I would be there. For me it was "love at first sight"—and very innocent.

Doug lived around the corner from my nana in Oshawa and, when I visited her, he came to her house to see me.

Rang the doorbell. I went to the door excited and thrilled, but glanced back nervously into the kitchen to see if my mother was watching. We stood under a tree by the sidewalk and talked. After that, he wrote me letters and sent me a small box of minerals because he knew I liked collecting rocks.

When his mother phoned my nana's house and asked if I could come for dinner, my mother practically flew round to their house to say, "She's only twelve! She is much too young for you to invite for dinner." I sat there, feeling small and ashamed, ready to sink through my chair.

My mother accused me of being "nervy" and "bold" without me knowing what those words meant. But the message was clear—I was a bad person. Within a month of the dinner invitation, I got a letter from Doug saying he was now interested in another girl. I never saw him again.

Why couldn't my mother simply have waited for adolescent ardor to dissipate, rather than label me with horrible names? I have no answer for that.

There was a stovepipe that came through the second floor of our house from the heater in the big kitchen where our family ate. It came up into the room that had been our chemical toilet room when we'd first moved to the country. It was now a storage room, where we kept Christmas decorations, winter coats, and old toys. This stovepipe was a conduit for whatever was being said downstairs by my parents. I could sneak soundlessly into the store room and listen to their conversations. As I grew older, this became more and more important to me—especially when I went to high school, was more interested in boys, and began to challenge my parents' restrictions.

I could hear my mother, "Going out with boys! She is too young to be thinking this way! I don't like the way she's acting. She looks more mature than she is and attracts boys that are way too old for her."

"Well, can't you just talk with her about that?"

"I'm going to warn her about what could happen if she rides in a car with a boy. Of course, not in detail. Explain that she can't go out with a boy—it's too dangerous and she could get into trouble."

"Okay, I'll let you handle this."

"Yes, you will."

As I think back on all this today, I can see that my mother was terrified of what most families in the fifties and sixties were afraid of—having a daughter that others might talk about and bring shame on the family—a daughter getting pregnant. (Petrie, A. 1998) Likely the same fears that her mother, my nana, lectured her and her sister about. At the time, all I knew was that I was a likely candidate for whatever would befall me if I got into a car alone with a boy—Mom warned me that my name would be "mud."

But she was afraid of the wrong things, and her fears—and her need to feel in control—kept her from simply sitting down and talking with me. My parents were more shocked and worried that I had normal feelings about boys my own age than that the girls in my elementary school were being pursued by an adult predator.

Although I could listen in and hear what my parents said via the stovepipe, I couldn't admit I had heard them. We just didn't talk.

Chapter 24
The Christmas Concert

Winter brought cold and excitement to our country village. When I started at Leskard school, the Christmas concert was held at the village church. As a Catholic, I was a bit nervous about being in a Protestant church, so Mom consulted our priest, who told her that, as long as I wasn't attending a church service, it was all right.

The next year the concert was moved to the upper classroom of the school—originally meant as a meeting or community room when the school was built in the 1860s, and before it became a classroom.

The Christmas concert was the big event of the year—and it took all of our fall school term to prepare for it. I was chosen by the Teacher to be the lead in the one act play—the centrepiece of the concert programme. We didn't try out for the parts—he assigned them. At eight years old—nearly nine—I was tall for my age and memorized things easily, so I was a natural choice for the lead part... I guess.

This was my first year in my new school and so far everything had been going well. I'd been accelerated to grade four, (instead of being in grade three). I was already used to being recognized for my abilities—my grade one teacher in Courtice had taken my workbooks to display at a teacher's conference, my grade two teacher in Oshawa had awarded me a prize for the highest marks in the class - so this all felt good and normal to me. However, when I interviewed Joan Gimblett, who'd attended school with the Teacher, she suggested there might have been a more calculated reason for the Teacher's attention toward me. How could I, or my parents, have known then how he felt about little girls?

Starting at the end of September, the Teacher called all the students chosen for the play up to the front of the classroom near the piano, while the other children worked on their lessons. Until the play was performed at each December concert, we would read the script and run through the lines and movements of the play until it was perfect. I loved the break from the tediousness of rote classroom learning.

I learned a few years later that the Teacher was part of an amateur theatre group in Orono, so possibly that was where he learned to stage plays. He asked if I wanted to join him in that theatre group (at age eleven). I loved acting and was thrilled at the prospect, but my mother said no. I remember walking to school, getting so angry that I was yelling out loud at my mother, who of course was not there to hear, for not letting me join.

Her reaction was totally understandable, though, and I knew that. In fact, given what we knew by that time about the Teacher, it would have been irresponsible to let me go. I would have been riding, in the evening, back and forth to Orono, alone, with the Teacher, in his car. But my mother didn't sit and talk with me about the reasons for her decision or why I was missing out on something I would have enjoyed. It just felt as though I was paying a price for the village's decision not to do anything about the Teacher.

* * *

The main choral numbers in the Christmas concert included all the children. We would line up at the front of the classroom according to size and musical parts—sopranos, altos and basses all standing together—smaller children in the front, tall ones like me in the back row. Smaller groups of singers practiced separately for their individual parts in the concert.

We practiced and practiced and practiced. And stood for what seemed like endless hours. During a particularly long practice in the upstairs classroom, the light around my vision began to close in and I saw black around the edges. The last thing I remember was lurching forward between two children standing in front of me. When my chin hit the floor, I lay in a heap, and the Teacher yelled to the other children to step aside.

Mr. Long, at that time the younger children's teacher, ran over and gently raised my head to see if I was all right. He saw the gash on my chin and realized I was going to have to see a doctor. Someone brought me a glass of water. I had never fainted before and had no idea that that was what had happened. When I felt less wobbly, I went to the cloakroom and dressed in my winter clothes—in slow motion. Mr. Long walked with me down into the valley, past the general store, and up the steep and slippery hills, to my house.

My mom dressed my baby brother and younger sister and gave Mr. Long a ride back down the hill to the school. Then she drove the ten miles to the emergency room of the Bowmanville district hospital where our family doctor was waiting. He stitched the cut.

The next day, I was back in school with a bandage on my chin, over the stitches. I remember the other students gathering around, asking me what had happened. No one seemed to know why I had passed out—perhaps it was just from standing for so long while we practiced—but the whole incident served to emphasize my vulnerability, my helplessness, in this new school environment.

* * *

We were divided into solo numbers, duets, and trios to sing the various numbers needed to round out the Christmas concert programme. The Gregory sisters sang together in a duet, and with Leslie Anderson, Diane Ball, and me for other numbers. Marilyn Gregory had a wonderful, clear singing voice that had won first prize at the music festival, so was chosen as the featured soloist. One day, during class, the Teacher asked Marilyn to stay in during recess and lunch hours until the concert to practice her numbers.

I looked from the Teacher to Marilyn and back again. Her face had a solemn look—she couldn't refuse to stay in, and she did have to rehearse, but I wondered why her practice couldn't happen during class hours—like the rest of us. I felt awkward for her but glad it wasn't me.

Each year, the Junior room teacher and our Teacher thought of new performances the children would do for the concert. The year I was in grade seven, Miss Cobbledick, the Junior teacher, taught a group of girls to shine flashlights in time to music. Another year, several of us demonstrated ballroom dancing.

When I spoke with my old classmate, Jill, over lunch in the Bowmanville Family Restaurant, she told me about what happened the year she, Diane Ball, Leslie Anderson, and Marilyn Gregory, were selected by the Teacher to do a majorette number. I remembered that performance when she talked about it, but didn't know what happened at the time.

The Teacher had taken Jill and the other girls aside to tell them his plan. They were to wear blouses and very short skirts to be made by Tillie Anderson, Leslie's mother and a seamstress in the village.

"Of course, we have to know what size skirt each of you'll need, so at recess, you girls will come upstairs so I can measure you."

It crossed Jill's mind that it would have made more sense for Mrs. Anderson to do the measuring, but, given her mother's warnings to obey the Teacher, she knew she didn't really have a choice. The girls stayed in for recess and climbed the steps to the second-floor classroom. The Teacher followed them.

When he was at the top of the stairs he said, "To have some privacy for the measuring, you girls can get into the storage cupboard and take off your clothes." Then he followed them in.

He put his hands on them—to figure out their skirt size, he said. There was a window in the storage room and Jill looked out, afraid someone outside would be able to see her without her clothes. She said she felt more concerned about that than what the Teacher was doing, because she knew there was no way she could prevent what was happening.

So many things had gone on under my nose. I sat listening to Jill at the restaurant table, my chest tightening, hardly breathing, feeling tears creep around my eyes as I realized how little I knew of all the Teacher's manipulations and how little protection girls in our school had. The majorette number was the hit of that year's concert.

* * *

Weeks ahead of each years' concert, we created advertising posters in art class. Our posters would be tacked onto bulletin boards in every general store in the surrounding villages, so they had to be perfect. Though, due to the informal "gossip telegraph" in the area, I doubted anyone really needed to consult the posters.

The upstairs classroom had to be decorated with a tree and crepe paper garlands. We sat at our desks and wound green, white, and red crepe paper into spirals and taped the ends so they wouldn't unroll. The Teacher told the bigger boys to go out to the tool shed and bring in a ladder so the garlands could be taped to the walls and windows. He also instructed them to set up the curtains for the stage.

Ricky Anderson and Bobby, the Gregory's' cousin, erected wire at the back of the upstairs room so cloth could be strung to form a stage with curtains. They tested the curtains to make sure they would slide back and forth easily for each of the numbers. Props for the play were placed off to the left in the storage room so they could be brought out and placed on stage before the play began.

The Teacher set up the ladder at the side of the upstairs classroom and called some of the girls to him. He handed them garlands and told them to climb the ladder. He said he would hand up the tape so they could attach them to the wall. When he saw nervous looks he told them not to worry because he would make sure they didn't fall.

According to one woman I interviewed, she said that, as one girl climbed up, the Teacher stood holding the ladder. He watched her every footstep. Touched her arm to reassure her. She climbed up, above the level of his eyes. He turned his head upwards and looked under her skirt.

"I saw him," my interviewee told me. "We all saw him; we said nothing. He touched her bare leg as she stood on the ladder."

The girl looked down at his face, at his hand on her leg, at the other children. What could she do? She taped the garland quickly and climbed down.

Then he called the next girl to climb up. Some he touched, some he didn't. He had preferences.

* * *

Every Christmas, my mother sewed a red dress for me—taffeta or velvet—to wear to the school concert, for church, and for Christmas day dinner at my nana's house. I loved the red taffeta one she made when I was eleven, almost twelve. I laid the dress out on my bed, put on my crinoline with the multiple lace layers, pulled the dress over my head, and smoothed the full skirt down over the crinoline. The stiff taffeta swished as I twirled in front of my dresser mirror to catch a glimpse of myself.

The night of the concert, the upstairs classroom filled with parents, including my mom and dad and baby brother, other children's younger sisters and brothers, grandparents, and neighbours—even families we normally never saw, like the Smiths. People arrived early so they wouldn't have to stand at the back.

I could feel the excitement as the full choir sang "Oh Come All Ye Faithful" to begin the concert. Numbers were announced and children filed onto the stage in turn to sing, recite poems, do impersonations, or dance. Then the one-act play began. Sometimes errors were made, whole sections performed in the wrong order, steps forgotten. Then we sang "Jingle Bells"—all verses—to end the concert. It was always a success—the culmination of months of work and the beginning of the Christmas season in our village.

A week or two before the concert, we had exchanged names in class for gift-giving so each child would have a present under the tree at the end of the concert. The Teacher gave out candy—chocolate-coated fondant, hard ribbon candy, candy canes—and the gifts—the gifts we children brought to exchange with each other, and those the Teacher had bought for each of us.

I now realize that giving the girls pricey gifts at other times of the year might have looked a bit odd, but no one could question the Teacher buying his students gifts at Christmas.

* * *

The year I was eleven and in grade seven, we girls received jewellery from the Teacher. I unwrapped my gift and opened the box. A necklace with a green faceted glass stone hung on a gold-coloured chain. I had never seen anything so fancy. Green like the forest where my Dad collected fiddleheads in the Spring—only clear, like the stream that ran through it. My classmate Janie got a necklace like mine, but with a bright robin's-egg blue stone. I watched as her sister Marilyn opened hers—a necklace with a large stone. It might have been purple, but I remember it being red. Red like Christmas, Santa's-suit red, but clear like a ruby I'd seen in pictures of the crown jewels.

We girls were receiving adult-style necklaces from a man dressed in a suit too tight for his bloated body, a bald toad of a man, a man that, by then, I had to force myself to look at.

As I stared at my necklace, I felt both thrilled and repelled at the same time—I so wanted to keep it, but knew I didn't want to wear this shiny, sparkly, beautiful thing.

When I tried it on at home, I held the chain away from my neck to make it stop irritating my skin. Finally, I took it off. I didn't want it touching me. It had come from *him,* and if he saw me wearing it, another part of me would belong to him.

I put the box with the necklace on top of my dresser. During the following week, I opened it again and again to stare at the bright clear stone. One day I closed my bedroom door, took the necklace out of the box, and put it on the floor. I hit it over and over, again and again, with the heel of my shoe, until the green stone popped out of the setting and the gold-coloured metal flattened. When spring came, I took the pieces of the necklace outside and buried them behind the garage.

* * *

Christmas in the country, in our family, had its magical moments. I remember walking back into the neighbours' Christmas tree plantation with my father to pick out our tree, chop it down, and bring it home. Often, we decorated it on Christmas eve so it stayed fresh longer. My brother's birthday is January first, mine January fifth, so we always left the tree up so we could open our birthday gifts under the tree.

The giant Eatons and Simpsons Christmas catalogues had come in the mail months before December so my sister and I had lots of time to go over each page carefully and pick out our most desired gifts. After I discovered that Santa was Mom and Dad, I went over my lists and wrote down the cost of each item, showing my mother that I was not asking for anything too expensive.

Christmas followed a predictable pattern. On Christmas morning, we children raced down the stairs at about five a.m. to see what Santa had left under the tree. We were only allowed to play with gifts that weren't wrapped, and Santa never wrapped his presents. When Mom and Dad got up, we opened our wrapped gifts, had breakfast, and got dressed in our best outfits to go to mass at St. Joseph's church in Bowmanville. The church would be packed and it was one of the few days a year when we all went to Mass together as a family. Dad didn't sleep in on Christmas morning. After Christmas Mass, we drove to Oshawa to my nana's house.

Aunt Dorothea and Uncle Walt came with my cousins, and some years Nana's brothers and their families piled into the house. Nana stood in the kitchen, supervising dinner preparations—turkey, mashed potatoes, rutabaga, peas, and gravy. Her homemade mincemeat pies sat on the kitchen table in anticipation of the end of the meal. Before the Christmas lunch, we sat in the living room and opened our gifts. They'd been placed under Nana's spruce Christmas tree, decorated with glass lights alive with bubbling water, and the old shiny silver and red ornaments she brought out every year. The silver foil "icicles" were recycled, as they were in our home.

The dining table was set with Nana's best silver and dishes, cut glass salt and pepper shakers, and sparkling glasses holding her famous homemade tomato juice. We all helped to ferry glass bowls filled with pickles, chutneys, and cranberry sauce from the kitchen—I could grab a pink or yellow fondant candy from on top of her buffet on the way.

Tradition said that a male member of the family had to carve the turkey—sometimes Dad and sometimes my uncle. The platter and bowls of vegetables were passed from one person to the next until they returned to the head of the table. Finally, the two large homemade mincemeat pies were carried from the kitchen as if they were royalty, and cut into slices that were topped with ice cream. As I grew older, I graduated from the children's table set up in the living room, to the dining room table, for the turkey dinner.

One year, Uncle Walt came into the kitchen holding a punch bowl filled with Aunt Dorothea's special Christmas punch—made with a splash of rum.

I can still hear Nana's shrill voice yelling at him, "You get that out of here right now! There is no alcohol allowed in this house." Nana's father had been an alcoholic, who, I learned through many iterations of the story, would leave home to go on a bender, then come home to impregnate Nana's mother—six times—and leave again. He drank away any money the family had and her mother had to scramble just to survive. When the money ran out, the children, including Nana, were put into orphanages until their mother could afford to retrieve them again. The youngest stayed in the orphanage so long she was adopted by another family and Nana had to search to find where she'd gone.

Uncle Walt took the bowl back out to their car. Even the adults drank ginger ale in Nana's house.

Late in the afternoon, after we'd eaten, Dad became the centre of attention. With an apron tied around his waist, he headed up the dishwashing crew in Nana's pantry—all of us standing with tea towels in hand to dry the newly-washed dishes. At home, Dad never helped with any of the "women's chores." I didn't know this father, the one that loudly announced at Nana's he would do the washing up on Christmas and New Year's, but I liked him better than the father I had at home.

When Nana got older and couldn't deal with the crowd, we alternated between Christmas or New Year's at Nana's and the other holiday at home. Too bad, because Nana's teetotal Christmas meant there was less chance Dad would drink too much on Christmas Day.

Chapter 25
Billy And The Training School

In addition to the issue with the Teacher, there were other forms of abuse going on, in and around the village. And no one wanted to address what went on. No one wanted to rock the boat.

Young Billy Churchill had been placed on the Bernston farm by the officials at the Bowmanville Training school—and the Bernston family was paid to keep him.

Knowing what I do now of Mr. Bernston, I can almost hear him yelling, "Shut up and get that pitchfork working—I don't give you food and a roof over your head so you can just stand around."

When Mr. Bernston raised his hand, Billy flinched. By that time, though used to the punishments Bernston doled out, he still hoped to avoid them.

Billy looked a bit younger than me—but he was in a grade ahead of me. I guess the Teacher thought he fit best there. He walked to school with the Bernston kids—Barbara, older than me, wide and tall—Mom called her "big-boned"—and Greg, her younger brother.

Many farmers in those days got boys from the Bowmanville Training School to work on their farms. They were considered free labour and the Training School viewed it as a good way to give the kids work experience. The village school whisperings said that all the boys at the Training School had something wrong with them. Billy was either an orphan or a criminal—or both. No one knew. The boys didn't live with their own families so they must be bad, even though Billy looked ordinary to me, not dangerous—sad really. The bullies in the school were the ones that seemed mean to me, which qualified them as bad boys in my mind, even though they lived with their own families.

Billy was young, so even though he worked on the farm, the law said he had to go to school. For the rest of us in class who were constantly dodging the menace of the older boys, it was a relief that they had another victim. Winter or summer, the big boys had school-yard tortures ready. Name-calling, grabbing, pinching, punching, pushing to the ground.

One day, one of the big boys took advantage of our largely unsupervised noon hours to call out, "Billy, you're just a trouble-maker, you know." Was he? Another boy, Brian, told me he considered him his best friend.

Billy gave the big boy a shove but then walked away. Later in the week, the teasing started again with, "Nobody wants you. That's why you're in that place."

One day, the arguing and fighting got to the point where the Teacher gave Billy a warning—"If you get into another fight, you'll get the strap."

I'd never had the strap, but my dad had warned me that if I ever got the strap at school, I'd get it again at home. I have no idea why Dad would say such a thing, as he knew I generally followed all rules and, besides, he never strapped us kids.

One week later, someone kicked Billy as he went out for recess. Billy waited and then grabbed the boy in the schoolyard. Punched him in the face. Someone went in and told the Teacher.

After we were back in the classroom ready to start our arithmetic assignments, the Teacher opened the bottom drawer of his desk and took out the strap. It was about a foot and a half long, and two and a half inches wide, made of rubber with some sort of material over it. Then he walked to Billy's desk. "Get up and go to the back of the classroom."

Billy got up from his seat and gave a sideways glance at the boy who had started the fight.

I kept my head down low, and tried to concentrate on the page of long division in front of me, but I peeked from under my arm that rested on the top of my desk, to the back of the room. I could see the Teacher, his large bulk towering over Billy.

"Hold out your hands."

Billy held out his small hands, brown with deeply ground-in dirt, calloused like a man's from tossing bales and raking cow manure, but with fingers barely bigger than my younger sister's.

I heard the first thwack onto Billy's hands. My ears clouded in at the second thwack, trying not to hear, trying not to imagine the red welts on the thin hands.

When the whacks stopped, the Teacher screamed at him that he was a trouble-maker and that he wouldn't have trouble-makers here. "You're expelled. Go to your desk, get your things, and GET OUT."

I could see then that he was a small boy, compared to the big boys in the class, but strong. He packed up his school bag and walked out the boys' door, never to return. If he couldn't go to school, the Bernstons would have to send him back to the Training School, where no parents would welcome him home.

* * *

The summer I was twelve, Leskard school was invited to play baseball at the Bowmanville training school with the boys who lived there. The sun was shining on a steaming June day. I sat on the grass, keeping score as I often did and looking carefully at the boys' faces as they played against my classmates. I knew they, like Billy Churchill, must be there because someone thought they'd done something bad, so I felt nervous, but I was old enough to wonder if the boys really *were* bad.

I wondered what Billy's fate had been when the Teacher expelled him from our school. When he returned to the Training School, was he sent for punishment in the "digger," where he would have to scrub floors on his hands and knees while being hit in the face and deprived of food? Some boys had reported that. One man I interviewed told me his uncle had worked at the Training School and used to "pound on the boys."

The digger was solitary confinement in a cell that contained only a mattress and a steel toilet—like an adult jail cell. It was for kids who couldn't control their emotions. Physical restraints were used when the boys were brought to the digger. They were let out for only one hour a day. The limit in the digger was officially three days, but, according to a former staff member, (who has asked that her name not be used) some boys always seemed to be there because they would "re-offend" right after being released from their cell, and then be sent back.

The most frightening thing reported by that former staff member was the "red blanket," though she personally never saw it happen—only heard about it. The victim was covered in a blanket and then beaten—until the blanket was red.

Many of the boys reported that, as adults, they were still plagued with nightmares, depression, and alcoholism due to the torture they endured. The threat of the "red blanket" sounded to me enough to induce nightmares.

Girls were sent to the Bowmanville Training School too and a woman who worked there in the seventies said few of the girls ever had visitors or even phone calls. However, she also said that in most cases the children came from families that lacked the financial means to visit their children, and long distance phone calls were expensive. She also said she didn't see any evidence of sexual assault, at least no child spoke to her about it, but most of the girls had been victims of sexual predators long before they reached the training school. In other training school locations, girls did suffer sexual and physical abuse—but if they tried to resist, were told no one would believe them if they said anything (The Toronto Star 5/4/2019). This was what the police told Cathy Spry's mother about the abuse going on at our school. In the 1950s and sixties, no one listened to young girls—not even the courts.

To date, two hundred and twenty lawsuits have been brought against the Ontario government for sexual, physical, and psychological abuse perpetrated by the staff in various training schools in Ontario—the very people charged with helping the boys who were incarcerated. At the time of writing, none of the lawsuits had been settled, according to the Toronto lawyer I spoke to who was working on the cases.

I have remembered Billy out of many children at our school whose faces I have forgotten over the years. The cruelty by both students and the Teacher that I witnessed is burned in my memory. Years later, Joan Lewis said that Billy had a "dog's life" on the farm with Howard Bernston. People knew, but nothing was done. It was no one else's business. That was just the way it was. Children just had to endure.

Chapter 26
Real Violence Happens In Toronto

Our home and property were across the road from the farm of Jim Smith and his family. We rarely saw Mr. Smith so I barely recognized him when he drove his pickup into our yard, parked, and came up the walk. When Dad went to the door, the two men stood and eyed each other. It was clear from my father's face that this was an unexpected visit, and no friendly chitchat began the conversation. I retreated to the living room so I could hear the whole exchange.

"I'm warning you, Roy, keep your dogs away from my farm."

"Okay, calm down, Jim. What's the problem?"

"I'll shoot your dogs if they come onto my property. I have the right to protect what's mine. And your dogs are chicken stealers."

"Wait a minute—you saw one of our dogs in the chickens?"

"No, but I don't have to. I saw blood in the coop and three of my chickens are dead. Feathers everywhere."

"Well, none of my dogs came home with feathers or blood on them."

"I don't care. Yours are the nearest dogs to me and I'm not losing any more chickens."

"Jim, we've been neighbours for years now. Surely this can be resolved differently. Maybe it was foxes or coyotes."

But Mr. Smith turned, walked down the steps of our porch, and yelled over his shoulder, "You mind what I said." He got into his truck and drove off.

Dad turned to my mother and said, "We're going to have to keep the dogs tied up. When there's really no reason to. But I'm not going to have them shot."

Dad had heard stories from some of the villagers about the Campbell's hound being shot dead. They couldn't prove it was Mr. Smith, but the dog was last seen running a wolf on the Smiths' farm. Dad wasn't going to take any chances. Hunting with our Brittany spaniels and fox hounds was my Dad's passion, but Smith saw the dogs as criminals.

"And we have to tell the kids not to go near the Smiths' property—you don't know what Jim is capable of."

They lived at the end of a very long narrow driveway, lined with so many trees the track seemed dark and impenetrable, like a forest track in my imagination, leading to a cottage covered with candy. My dad didn't have to worry, I was too scared to ever venture near their farm. What if Mr. Smith saw something moving and shot before finding out what it was? I couldn't see the house or barn from the main road, and never went with my Dad when he drove over to appeal to Mr. Smith's "neighbourliness."

We only ever saw Mrs. Smith in the passenger seat when we passed their pickup truck on the road, or when it was parked at the General Store while Mr. Smith went in for groceries or the mail. The only village social event they attended was the annual school Christmas concert—the only time I saw their faces close up. Mr. Smith's expression was grimness set in concrete; Mrs. Smith's face was sad, her eyes always looking as though they were about to drip tears.

Mom told me one day that Mrs. Smith had taken her children to her mother's up near Millbrook. She added,

"Mr. Smith must be a difficult man. I don't think he lets her go anywhere."

I'd never heard of a woman leaving her husband, but in a few weeks the children, Hazel and Peter, were back in school as though nothing had happened. About two years later it happened again—they were gone, but back again after a month.

After Mom told me this, I stared all the more when I saw the Smiths together. This was what an unhappy family looked like.

Possibly my Mom visited when she was selling Avon. In the country, Avon representatives, as they were called, had to drive to each potential customer—maybe Mom used that as an excuse to satisfy her curiosity about the Smiths, their house, and their marriage, but she never said.

Hazel Smith was near my age but a bit younger. Her brother Peter was in my sister's class. Sometimes they would walk to school with Bonnie and me if we happened to pass their laneway at the time they were starting their walk to school. They were very quiet children—rarely looked at us or talked as we walked. I guess we got used to that because we didn't question it. I never knew them—not really.

After I left home to go to university, Mom updated me about the family. Mrs. Smith and Hazel eventually left the farm for good, but Peter stayed to work with his father. He found his father one morning, dead in bed. Peter worked the farm alone until he died—in his early fifties. I never did see their house or barn, but the township named the road nearest to their property after them.

* * *

I learned so much about the village and other surrounding villages when I did my interviewing. Mrs. Rollins, who lived in Orono, the nearby town where Reverend Long lived, was beaten by her husband on a regular basis—not something anyone would call the police over. It was "their business," a domestic matter, not violence. Real violence was something you saw on television or read about in the Toronto newspapers.

A woman who lived on a farm near our village disappeared. Never to return. The rumour was that her husband threw her down the well. You would think the police would have checked that one out, but maybe no one reported the woman as missing. She was just gone. Run away? Maybe. No one really knew. It was not something anyone would get involved with except to talk about.

Children were beaten in families, but it wasn't called abuse. Brian Buckley said it was just the way parents taught children right from wrong back then.

* * *

Another rumour in the village was that Ricky Anderson's mother came after her sons with pots and pans. Hit them in the head. I was soon to find out if this was true.

Leslie Anderson was the youngest child in the family, with four older brothers. Ricky was in the same grade as me, nervous, sweet and quiet, often doing impersonations to make us all laugh. Danny was older than Ricky so I barely knew him. The two oldest brothers had already left school to work.

Mom wanted me to take skating lessons like she had when she grew up in Oshawa. The closest place with an arena was Orono, about five miles away. Mom signed me up for lessons and Mrs. Anderson signed Leslie up. For two weeks in a row in the winter, when Dad was on days and the car was at home, I walked home, and then, after supper, Mom drove me down to the village to pick Leslie up so we could both go to skating lessons. Mrs. Anderson drove us into Orono the weeks when Dad was on nights, so I walked to Leslie's home after school on those days.

That's how I found out that the rumours were true—Mrs. Anderson *did* hit her sons over their heads with pots and pans. I saw it happen. She didn't try to hide it.

One week it would be Danny, the next it might be Ricky being chased around the house by their mother—with a cooking pot in her hands. I prayed it wouldn't make contact.

Mrs. Anderson was gossiped about, the gossip mulled over, shared over and over, possibly even laughed about. According to one villager, Mrs. Anderson was "wild as a March Hare." It wasn't child abuse—it was something amusing to most people—and, just how it was.

* * *

We knew that Billy Churchill was beaten by Mr. Bernston. He had shown his bruised and bloody back to Brian. Mr. Bernston's vicious temper was known throughout the village. One day when Jean, a village woman, went into labour, she lifted the phone, but someone came on the party line before she had a chance to call her mother or the doctor. A voice told her, "We've got an emergency here. Got to call the doctor." Jean hung up and tried again fifteen minutes later, figuring someone else must have an emergency more pressing than impending birth. But later she found out the true story. Someone needed to call the vet. Mr. Bernston had beaten his horse so badly, it was dying, and the neighbours were trying to save it. It was too late, though. The horse died.

* * *

Cruelty in the village took forms other than physical violence. I was taunted for being Catholic—something I didn't know was a problem until we moved to the country. The whole area had been settled by Irish Protestants, many of whom had a long-standing hatred of Catholics. There had been Orange parades in our village, in Kendal, and in Orono in the past and there were still Orange Lodges in some of the villages. The prejudices still remained. But there was racial intolerance, too.

"You're an Indian," one of the bullies yelled at Margie as she and I were leaving the schoolyard to walk home. She didn't say anything and soon we were talking about comics—love comics were my favourites after Superman and Supergirl comics. Margie was only a year older than me, but twice her family had left the area. Each time they left, she went to school in Toronto, so she seemed much older than me. Older and braver—I could never have yelled out my dislike of the Teacher in class like she'd done.

When I got home that day, I said to my Mom, "One of the kids yelled at Margie today. He said she's an Indian."

Mom hesitated... then a minute or so later, responded, "Well, you're part Indian."

Wait, what? Really? No. I don't think so. I stopped in my tracks—I had never heard this story before. In fact, both Mom and Dad repeatedly talked about our ancestry being Irish on both sides of my family. I thought about this while my mother continued her cleaning.

After I'd spent an hour pondering, Mom approached me, "No, you are not part Indian. But, did you feel any different? When I told you that you were?"

"No." No, I didn't, but on the other hand, I still didn't know what an Indian was.

Years later, I've come to realize that likely my mother didn't want me to be prejudiced against anyone different from myself. Her mother, my nana, was prejudiced against black people—in fact Nana once told me that the only black person she liked was Lesley Uggams who sang on the Lawrence Welk show. I knew she would never rent one of her boarding house rooms out to a black man, no matter how polite. Possibly not to an Indian either?

I didn't feel different from Margie—she was just a girl in my class who gave me rides on her bike. Was she an Indian? I didn't know. And what was that, anyway? Our family had been to the reconstructed Huron Indian village in Midland, near the Martyrs' Shrine, but as a young girl I couldn't connect that to anyone real, anyone living. And we didn't learn much in school about First Nations people.

I didn't know why Margie moved away several times and lived in Toronto. Did her family have the same problems as the Smiths across the road? Problems so bad that the wife left several times and then came back again before finally moving for good? I had no idea.

My dad had gone to St. Michael's College in Toronto—a private Catholic boys' school right in the heart of downtown. He hated being away from home but his mother couldn't keep him out of trouble so his uncle said he had to go—he and his brother. Dad told stories of when he was at school in Toronto—about how, when he ran out of money by month end, he would walk to the downtown pawn shops and pawn his watch until Granny sent him more spending money. Then he could redeem his watch until he again needed more money. He had freedom in his teen years that I could only dream about—and in Toronto.

While growing up, I only visited Toronto twice, though it was only fifty miles away. Once, when my parents took me to the St. Lawrence Market, I saw foods I had never heard of before—pickled vegetables, black olives, and whole coconuts with the milk still inside! It all seemed so magical and exotic to me. Though we didn't usually eat out, that one time we ate at a restaurant in Chinatown.

When Margie and her family were living in Toronto, did she have the same freedom as my dad had? Did she eat black olives and pickled vegetables? She seemed so much more worldly than me, she *must* have gone to the St. Lawrence Market. For me, it would only be after I finished university when I married my first husband that I finally lived in magical Toronto.

* * *

While much violence already existed in this rural area, my father brought his own bad habits to the country, the behaviour his uncle had tried to change

"Mom, there's a police car in the driveway—and he's coming to the door with Dad."

The police officer opened the door and both he and my father stepped into the house. The officer introduced himself and Mom invited him into the living room. I sat in the big kitchen, not wanting to miss any of the story. Dad had been driving east over the top of Hardy's hill and saw a car that had slid crosswise on the ice on the hill. There was no way Dad could avoid crashing into the side of the car.

I could see my father's puffy lips and hear him slur his words when he spoke, but Dad's drinking was never mentioned. No charges were laid—the policeman said the accident was unavoidable. He couldn't have steered clear of the other car. Drunk driving was against the law, whether you hit someone or not, so I never knew why the police didn't press charges. Possibly, if Dad had been charged, it would have proven to him that he needed to stop drinking so much, but it didn't happen.

One of the men from the village that I interviewed said to me, "We all drank back then—and drove. I did. Until I sobered up. Your dad, he drove drunk."

I stayed silent at first, not wanting to admit this, even after all these years, then answered, "Yes, I knew that." Of course I knew, but I'd been naive. I didn't think other villagers had seen that side of my father. I thought he'd successfully maintained the image he so wanted to portray.

* * *

Now we have names, even laws, for some of the things I saw and heard about in the village—child abuse, racism, drunk driving, domestic violence, cruelty to animals—but back then, none of these things were generally considered something you called the police for. They were private, domestic issues—no one else's business. It was the way life was. So why should I be surprised that nothing was done about a pedophile teacher?

Chapter 27
Escape Is Imminent—I Turn Thirteen

The prospect of turning thirteen loomed large in my mind. I must have carried the illusion that, as a teenager, things would change for me in my family, in the village, at the school.

I desperately wanted to have a birthday party. The last party I'd had was when I turned eight while we still lived in Courtice.

"You're not having a party."

"Why?" I was just arguing—not really interested in her reasons.

"I just don't want you to have a birthday party," Mom said.

"But why?" I was on the verge of tears.

"Because when you have a party on your birthday, you're begging for presents."

"Please. I just want to have a party when I turn thirteen. It's special. I won't ask for any other party."

"No, I don't want a party in this house."

"I'll tell them not to bring any gifts."

She frowned, so I could tell she still hadn't changed her mind... but she gave in.

I went to school and invited all my friends—everyone in grades seven and eight and some from grade six. I told them not to bring presents.

"You have to do all the preparation yourself. I'm not going to help."

When we went shopping, I bought chips and pop.

The night of the party, I had a bath in the four inches of water we were allowed to use, with a few drops of "Somewhere" fragrance bath oil Mom sold as an Avon representative. I slipped on my new mauve polished-cotton dress.

I pushed back the chairs in the living room in case we decided to dance—which I longed to do. It was 1962 and I pictured a scene straight out of Dick Clark's American Bandstand—smiling, laughing, energetic teenagers twirling each other on the dance floor. I got out my small record collection—two 78 rpm records by Ricky Nelson, "Lonesome Town" and "Travelling Man," some 45s, "Telstar" by the Tornadoes, and "The Twist" by Chubby Checker, and an LP my cousin had given me for Christmas, of pop songs covered by unknown bands. At the last minute, I applied the new pale pink lipstick my parents had given me for my birthday—and waited for my magical evening to begin.

As soon as the first person came I knew I was in trouble—she brought a present. In fact, all my friends brought presents. Either no one believed my mom wouldn't allow them, or, more likely, their parents thought it was odd going to a birthday party without a gift. I piled them up on our dining table and tried to be gracious—but I knew I would pay a price later.

The second problem was I hadn't planned anything for us to do except dance—and none of the boys wanted to dance. I put on "The Twist" and most of the girls got up and danced in the centre of the room. The boys sat on the couch or the chairs, or stood around watching us. I halted the dancing for a few minutes when some of the girls urged me to open my presents: Evening in Paris perfume, bubble bath, a scarf, a tiny pin to wear on a sweater, and a box of candy.

Of course, there were the popular girls, the cute girls, and the awkward girls—all came, but some were more at ease than others. Janie with her golden hair and her sister Marilyn with red curly hair were slim and good-looking. Shirley was overweight, with a large round red face and huge hair that stood out so stiffly she could barely tame it with barrettes.

Mid-way through the evening, some older boys came to the door—boys who had gone to our school but were now in high school. They were bored. Nothing much to do in our village. Someone had told them there was a party, so they showed up at our house. I felt as though I had to let them in. They drank pop, ate chips and began to make fun of Shirley, the big girl. They shoved each other with their elbows, laughing and punching one another in the arm as they made obvious—and insulting—references to Shirley's size. She sat stone-faced on the couch. Perhaps she had endured this before. It didn't matter who started it—I was the host of the party and it was my responsibility to stop the teasing. I watched Shirley get more and more upset while I felt more and more embarrassed and helpless.

Then my mother came downstairs to supervise. She called me into the kitchen. "WHAT'S going on?"

Tears formed in the corners of my eyes.

"That's it—this party is over. You tell everyone they have to leave."

I was relieved in a way, because things had gone badly—but I needed help, not the reaction I got from my mother. I went back into the living room to tell my friends to go home.

After they left, she yelled, "That's it! I told you not to let them bring presents, and you should have had more for them to do—like games."

In retrospect, games sounded like a good idea, but I didn't realize that before the party or even while it was going on. I was a failure and so ashamed that, at thirteen, I couldn't manage something as simple as a party. It all looked so easy on the Adventures of Ozzie and Harriet as Ricky Nelson's friends gathered in their living room while Ricky sang "Lonesome Town." Television teenagers led golden lives.

* * *

By the time I had turned thirteen, in grade eight, I didn't feel challenged at Leskard school, so I looked elsewhere for things to read to excite my interest. Reading occupied such a large part of my life that my parents signed me up for membership in the Bowmanville Library. Mom warned me to sign out only one book at a time so it would be finished by the time it was due to be returned. I read my book the first night I had it. Then I looked for another book in our house to read.

"Read your library book," Mom said.

"I did already."

"What! You finished already? Now what are you going to do? You should have read a few pages each day, spaced it out."

But it was a Nancy Drew mystery!

My Nana had a copy of *Gone with the Wind* and I started to read it when I visited her—then asked to take it home. I read it all in one day and night. Later I borrowed a copy of *Wuthering Heights* from the Bowmanville library, and also read it non-stop. These were the perfect romance novels for me—young women in the country, longing for love with handsome, dark-haired, moody men.

The Teacher kept reminding our class how difficult high school was going to be, so I wanted to be prepared. I read the copy of Shakespeare's *The Merchant of Venice* I found on our school library shelves, and studied a French primer designed for grade nine.

The Teacher gave me catalogues so I could order books for the school library—a job he should have done, but I was thrilled to be given this responsibility. I ordered ones I wanted to read—*The Moonstone,* a mystery book by Wilkie Collins, and other books that sounded intriguing, like *We of Nagasaki.* I had never before read anything about World War Two and the dropping of the atomic bomb on Japan.

I knew that escape from elementary school and the Teacher was imminent—after the coming summer, I would go to high school.

* * *

In September 1962, when I was thirteen and a half, I walked down our country road—but only to the General Store where the school bus picked up the students from the village to go to Clarke High school, on Highway 115, just south of Orono.

I had dreamed of that day—escape from the village, its school and the Teacher. I was partially right to think that this was an escape. At the high school, there were many teachers, not just one, and interesting classes and clubs to join. A whole new world. There were teachers who seemed to care about their students, not to exploit them, but to encourage them. Other students didn't know about—or speak about—our school, or our Teacher. I could put it all behind me.

Now I know that escape is only an illusion. You never really break free from what we girls went through, but I didn't know that then. A study published in 2017, looking at outcomes in sexually abused victims, showed that "being a girl was a predictor of post-traumatic stress symptoms." (Gauthier-Duchesne, Hebert & Daspe, 2017)

* * *

Growing up, to me, meant making my own decisions, so I tried to negotiate that with my mother.

"Instead of getting my usual allowance, could I get two dollars a week and I'll buy my own clothes?"

After a discussion with my father, she agreed, but the following week, she brought home a yellow wool winter coat for me. She had seen it on sale in Eatons and loved it.

I liked the coat too, but I looked at it and said, "I can't afford it. Please take it back."

She was stunned, and argued with me, but she did take it back. From that time, I sewed as many of my clothes as I could, saved my money, used summer job money, and bought clothes on sale.

Now that I think back on this, I realize that taking over the decision-making about my own clothes interfered with one of the household jobs my mother took very seriously, and possibly gave her a sense of importance.

My father wouldn't let my mother work, but she looked after the financial ledger in our house. I think Mom and Dad must have agreed early on in their marriage that, because she had been a stenographer in a bank, she should handle the family money. At least once a month, she sat in the living room, the huge black ledger open on the couch, while she transferred the amounts from store receipts to the book. She recorded every cent spent—even twelve cents for a package of gum was written down. Dad had an allowance for beer and cigarettes. Before I was born, Dad had put most of his inheritance into a delivery business that failed, so perhaps that made it imperative that Mom handle the family money.

Over time, Dad was promoted at the Motors—to foreman, to line inspector, to general inspector for safety—so his salary increased. There was more disposable cash. He continued over the years to hand his pay cheque to Mom to pay all the bills and keep track of his income. She even filled out his income tax return. I am sure they jointly discussed large expenditures like the new bathroom, kitchen appliances, or when they fixed up the bedroom for my sister and me, but other than that, Dad displayed little interest in Mom's ledgers as long as he had his beer and cigarettes, and money for his hunting trips.

* * *

The year I started high school, 1962, the movie *Lawrence of Arabia* was released. My mother took me to see the movie, so she did listen sometimes and try to do what I wanted. Of course, I was immediately infatuated with Peter O'Toole and Omar Sheriff, and was drawn to the desert, though I didn't go to Egypt, Lebanon, and Syria until I was in my forties.

But thirteen days into October 1962, was also the time of the Cuban Missile crisis. All the world held its breath to see if the Russians would pull their nuclear warheads out of Cuba. John F. Kennedy, the United States President at the time, made it clear that they had to, or there would be war.

I was terrified but also practical. Where would we go if a bomb dropped? I looked at pictures of bomb shelters in magazines like *True, the Man's Magazine* that my father left in the bathroom. I read about outfitting a shelter, and bombarded my parents endlessly with questions about it.

"Where will we go if a bomb drops?"

"Do you have a plan?"

"Do we have a shelter? A bomb shelter?"

I was frightened and couldn't let it go. I watched the news on television and came away with estimations about how long my family and I could survive a nuclear war even if we had a very well-equipped shelter.

I'd read about the United States dropping atomic bombs on two cities in Japan at the end of the Second World War, and couldn't get the images from *We of Nagasaki* out of my head. People, their skin black and hanging off their bodies, stumbled around after the blast. Over two hundred thousand killed immediately or as a result of the bombs. It horrified me to think about what they'd gone through.

President Kennedy urged Americans to build bomb shelters, and drills were being held in schools in the United States. Children were to go under their desks if a bomb was about to drop. But what were *we* doing?

Finally, Mom said we could use the old cistern behind the barn if anything were to happen. The cistern was large, rectangular, and half-buried in the dirt—originally a storage container to hold runoff rainwater for farm animals to drink. It had been poured a long time ago from dark-coloured, coarse cement, possibly in the mid-1800's when the farm was established and the house built. It looked solid, its surface not cracked or too worn. But I never saw the inside of it, so how could I be sure this space would be adequate? Were there air filters? Would it be warm in the winter, stocked for the months and months of habitation that would be needed after a nuclear attack when radiation levels would be too high to exit?

My parents said we could equip the cistern *if* there was a Russian attack. Wouldn't that be too late? I don't think they seriously thought this was a good plan—they said it only to shut me up. They had made no preparations, stored no cans of food, blankets, containers of water, heaters, or lights. The cistern only had small openings for the barn's downspouts to fit into. How would we even get into it?

After thirteen days, the missile crisis was averted when Khrushchev agreed to pull the Russian nuclear weapons out of Cuba.

Many years later in university, I stayed alone in my residence for reading week. I didn't want to go home, so I told my parents I had papers to write. Instead, I read *On the Beach*. I knew then that our cistern bomb shelter would never have protected us from anything. But by then, the Cuban missile crisis was long over.

Chapter 28
Life With My Parents

When I first went to high school, I did well in my subjects. I did my homework diligently, joined the Glee Club, the folk club, and the library assistants' group where I learned to check books in and out of the library. I had always been terrible at sports so I didn't try out for basketball or volleyball. The teachers liked me because I worked hard, participated in class, and was well-behaved. They complimented my parents on how "mature" I was. They didn't know I was angry. But neither did I.

For much of my childhood, I was able to compartmentalize—I knew who to be polite to, who to listen to, who to obey. No rebellion or teenage histrionics for me. But as I got older, I couldn't stop my emotional compartments from spilling into one another. I didn't know why I was so sarcastic with some of my classmates. When one of the girls turned to me to make a harmless comment, I snapped at her, and watched the look on her face change from shock to dislike. I had no idea how to treat people, or how to make friends. But I watched and slowly I learned.

Like Schrodinger's cat, I was both miserable and happy at the same time, tucked away in my box until such time the top was opened to determine which I really was—and neither my parents nor I dared to do that.

* * *

The first Christmas after I started high school, my parents gave me a transistor radio—brown leatherette with a handle and a shiny gold-coloured front. Every night, I sat at the desk my mother had painted blue that stood in front of my bedroom window. As I did my homework, I tuned in to 1050 CHUM, the most popular Toronto pop station in the "Greater Toronto Area." You could even pick up the "CHUM Chart," twenty miles away in Wilson's, an Oshawa music shop. I rode the invisible highway of radio waves to the big city and connected to what other young girls like me were listening to. That small box was my gateway to the outer world.

Eventually I made new friends in high school. My best friend, Liz, lived on Highway 2 east of Newcastle. She seemed older and more mature than the rest of our classmates. Her father died when we were in grade ten, leaving her, her mother, and sister to run the gas station and snack bar they owned. Much more responsibility than I had. I spent many Saturdays just hanging out at her home. In grade eleven, she and I were both on the Student Council. I was the secretary, Liz was in charge of entertainment. I helped her with dance decorations, and bought new 45 records for the school dances.

We decided to sing together, and for our first performance—at one of the high school dances—sang "Red Roses for a Blue Lady," a hit song by Bobby Vinton, accompanied by an instrumental version of the record. After that, we were invited to sing at a variety show being held on May 12th, 1965, in the Newcastle Town Hall. I was headed for stardom, I was sure.

I guess I really hadn't consciously been pay attention to the trouble that existed between my mother and father until the night Liz and I sang in Newcastle. Dad drove me to the town hall and, waving goodbye, said, "I'll be back at eleven to pick you up."

Liz and I wore the matching blue dresses we'd ordered from the Eaton's catalogue for the performance, with red roses pinned to our shoulders—and sang our song for the audience. Then I waited outside on the sidewalk in front of the town hall for my Dad.

He wasn't alone when he drove up to the curb. A woman was with him, sitting next to him, her arm over his shoulder. We weren't introduced. I looked at the woman and back at my father, this father I knew but suddenly didn't know. I saw his familiar puffy lips and heard him slur his words. I had seen my father drunk many times, but drunk and flirting? I'd never seen this side of him. I knew he shouldn't be driving when he was so obviously inebriated, but I couldn't refuse to get into the car. I couldn't criticize him. Without ever having been told, I knew Dad's drinking was a forbidden topic in our family.

I sat in the back seat as Dad drove out of Newcastle and turned north onto Highway 115. This was long before the government did anything about the multiple car crashes, rear-enders, and fender-benders that took many lives on Highway 115. There were no seatbelts in the car, so I sat up, holding on to the back of the front seat. Tensed. Ready for a wreck. Waiting to die. There was nothing else I could do.

The woman's hair brushed my father's shoulder as she lengthened her arm to encircle his neck and snuggle closer. She talked to my father in a way that made me uncomfortable, like I'd felt years before when the boy next door used to visit my mother.

We drove into our driveway and I got out of the car. My mother opened the side door and barely seemed to touch the ground as she ran past me, opened the car door, and screamed at my father. The other woman just sat there. My father said nothing. He reached out, pulled the car door shut, and drove off down the laneway.

My mom then realized I was there and screamed, "Get into the house. NOW!" *What had I done?*

This had been a special night for Liz and me, yet my parents never asked how things had gone, or even acknowledged our accomplishment.

The story of what had happened gradually came out. After Dad had dropped me off in Newcastle, he hadn't gone straight home. A neighbour on the next farm from us was having a party, so he decided to drop in, drink way too much beer, and pick up a strange woman—though that part was never discussed.

He returned home in the middle of the night and slept in the spare room. He was still there when it was time for Liz and me to go to Bolton Camp, a children's camp north of Toronto, to be camp counsellors for two weeks.

I worried the whole time I was away—were my parents going to be together by the time I got home? Would they get a divorce? I became so sick I had to go into the nurses' cabin where I was shot with penicillin.

When I got home, Dad had moved back into their bedroom. Mom and Dad acted as though nothing had happened. Neither of my parents ever spoke to me again about what had happened that night.

Many arguments like this, for all different reasons, occurred while I was still living at home, before I finished high school and went to university. After my mother flew into another rage and got out of the car to go to her mother's, with me in the back seat, I suggested to my father that maybe they should consider marriage counselling. He flung a loud "shut up" over his shoulder, and drove off in a huff with me rendered silent. Later that day, we went back to Nana's to pick Mom up, after she had calmed down.

That evening, Dad came to my bedroom and told me that he and Mom were fine, all was well, they loved each other, no counselling needed. Case closed. No further discussion necessary. My father had spoken.

I said nothing. I heard him, but didn't believe a word of it.

* * *

Several years earlier when my mother had expressed her fears about me and boys, she had been right. Once in high school, I attracted the attention of an older boy. I was fourteen. Bob was seventeen, in grade eleven, and old enough to drive.

Mom was livid. "You're too young to have an older boy interested in you."

I wasn't allowed to date so we met at the school dances and the local highway restaurant.

Our high school arranged trips every year to Stratford to see the Shakespearian plays. When I was in the tenth grade, Bob and I both went to Stratford. We walked and talked, ate lunch in a restaurant, and went to the play. Back home, Mom asked me whom I'd spent the day with. I should have lied, but that wasn't me. When I said his name, she yelled, "ALL DAY? You spent ALL DAY with him?" I was in trouble.

"You are so nervy," she said and walked away.

I didn't know what that meant, except that I was a bad person, a shameful person who did shameful things. I couldn't go out on dates with Bob. I was too young. Eventually he avoided me. I cried angry, frustrated tears.

* * *

After I'd been in high school for about two years, a huge rumour hit the rural "verbal news telegraph." A girl in the village was pregnant—with the Teacher's baby.

Joan, a woman I interviewed who didn't even live in the village, heard the story from her parents. The girl was from a poor family who rented their property. According to Joan, the girl looked sad, dejected, poorly nourished. Villagers were certain the rumour was true. The Teacher molested girls, so this also had to be true.

Another woman described it as an affair—not rape—an affair between a young teenage girl and a grown man. Someone else said the girl had a boyfriend who most likely fathered her child; others said there was no boyfriend. But few questioned the rumour that the Teacher had done this.

Around that same time, a girl in the village said her sister was pregnant and the Teacher had come to their house several times to meet with their parents. He gave them money to help with her sister's travel expenses.

A girl did drop out of school and leave the area for a while, possibly to go to live with a wealthy Toronto family, be a nanny, and give up her baby for adoption. That's what young, single, pregnant girls did back then. (Petrie, A. 1998)

In the village where I lived, a Teacher was teaching young girls—including my own sister—that many believed was capable of impregnating one of his own students.

As I looked back on all this, the realization that my parents were really no different from any other village parents who had sent their children to this school came as a shock to me. My mother had always regarded herself as "different," more aware, better than the other villagers. Perhaps she thought that because she didn't deny the Teacher's behaviour, she was more intelligent than the other families, the other mothers. But while she didn't deny it as Jill's mother had, she disavowed the effects that having a pedophile teacher could have on her daughters. And my father went along with her.

But it didn't matter how horrifying all this was—when I was in high school, I didn't have to think about it anymore. I had escaped. I could put on a nice dress and matching sweater, apply my pale pink lipstick, put on a "good face," and do my school work. It was not my problem anymore.

* * *

As time went by, I resented my mother more and more. I listened more at the stovepipe. Heard her tell my dad how terrible I was. At times, I openly and rudely insulted her, while still obeying her.

I tried to keep up with my homework in high school and do well. In grade eleven I was chosen to go to the mini-United Nations at Queen's University, Kingston. I think my parents allowed me to go because my grandparents lived in Kingston, and I could visit them. But while there, I realized how out of touch I was with girls my own age. They seemed so relaxed, so friendly, so confident, so at ease, and they knew about sex and boys.

In grade twelve, I was chosen by my science teacher to attend a two-week science summer school at McMaster

University in Hamilton. It was a big honour to be chosen. My parents refused to let me go. I never knew why. I had to go back to school and tell my teacher, who was stunned at the news. I stayed home that summer and never did find out who went in my place.

That same summer, several of my classmates applied to work at the Banff Springs Hotel, in Alberta. I desperately wanted to go. Again, my parents said no. My mother told me that my father had talked to men who worked with him in GM. They said young girls who worked at the hotel were expected to act as prostitutes for businessmen who were guests at the hotel. Of course, even at the time I knew that was ridiculous, and I didn't know if my father had said that or not. Perhaps my mother lied because she simply didn't want me to go. Whatever the reason, my parents had decided. I wanted to rebel, argue back, shout, and scream, but my father and mother had so much power over me, I just couldn't.

In retrospect, I realize that my parents' restrictions were just a way to stop me from going—anywhere. I never really knew who wanted to restrict me more, my mother or my father, but I knew that Dad didn't want my mother to do anything outside our house either. Also, many years later, my aunt, my father's younger sister, said that Dad had done the same thing to her. Controlled where she could go to university. In retrospect, she thought it was funny. But I didn't. My father was unreasonable and domineering, and it hadn't started with my mother and me.

To avoid my parents' disapproval and lessen the ongoing sense of guilt I lived with, I began to restrict myself. I turned down invitations to ordinary teenage events in anticipation of my parents' wishes that I not do anything outside our house. I stayed home, yearning for escape. Yearning to make my own decisions.

At the time, I didn't put together my parents' control of my behaviour with the hypocrisy they were still engaged in regarding the Teacher—my sister was still being taught by him and they continued to do nothing. Like me, she knew what he was doing, what he was capable of, but couldn't get away either. We weren't allowed to.

When I was seventeen, in grade twelve, I was too anxious to sleep or do homework—shaking, crying, panicking, depressed. My mother took me to the doctor to have me checked out medically, but her "big cure" was to take me to Yorkdale Shopping Centre in Toronto. Mom must have discussed this with Dad, because she had a set amount of money she allowed me to spend. I picked out a light blue angora sweater with short sleeves, and some pearl earrings. Retail therapy, just the thing to fix anxiety and depression. Counselling or talking therapy was not popular in the sixties so it was not even an option for me or my parents—in fact I have no idea if it was even discussed—and it was years and many sessions of therapy later before I recognized I'd had a nervous breakdown.

When I was much older, I began to put together how my parents dealt with Dad's depression and anxiety and their frustrations about life. When family would come over, and then years later when grandchildren visited, Dad could only stand so much togetherness. After an hour or so he would get up from his chair saying, "Well, that's enough, I've got to get out of here." He would either drive off or walk into the fields. No one commented, no one knew why he was like this, and he didn't talk about it. But the doctor gave him medication to calm his tension—and he drank.

Drugs, alcohol and cigarettes—that's how Dad coped. Now, I think he might have had post-traumatic stress disorder, but whether it was from his father dying suddenly when he was seven, or from living with his mother who also calmed her nerves with alcohol, I will never know. Early in his life he kept his drinking and work separate, but in later years, the booze leaked into every day. He would drink a beer before the night shift or read the newspaper with a scotch in his hand, leaving only a few days in the middle of the work week when he was somewhat sober.

My aunt, my father's sister, who was a nurse, took me aside one day when she was visiting. I was in my twenties by then. "I'm worried about the number of drugs both your parents are taking," she said.

I listened and empathized with her concern, but could do nothing about it. Perhaps I had just stopped caring. My parents were stuck in their ineffective methods of dealing with issues—not communicating about problems, rather, medicating and then living on hope things might change.

I had a boyfriend in my last year of high school. Grant was kind, thoughtful, took me to events like hockey and baseball games, the Ice Capades, and formal dances, and asked me to marry him. I told him I was too young to make that kind of decision, but really, I knew he was not the man for me.

I finished grade thirteen with high enough marks to be accepted at any university I wanted—including the University of Toronto—but chose Trent, in Peterborough, because it was close to home. So, when given a choice, I chose safety over exotic Toronto.

Chapter 29
Leskard School Closes

In 1967, the year I finished high school, all the country elementary schools in Ontario were closed by the Department of Education, and the buildings and land sold to the highest bidders. Most were turned into homes. But Leskard School was closed in 1966, a year before the new regional school in Kirby was ready, so the children, including my brother, went to various other country schools for a year before they were bused to Kirby. Why was our school treated differently, I wondered?

One of the villagers I spoke with, whose family had moved into the village after I'd started high school, said he was aware that the Teacher was "too friendly" with the girls in the classroom. I spoke with Shelley Beattie who lived just south of the village about what had happened to her.

Shelley had a beautiful singing voice and won three awards for her solo performances at the local music festival. When she was in grade six, she was standing in the classroom to sing and the Teacher put his hand on her chest to show her and the class how to use the diaphragm in singing—then he moved his hand down, down, down until it was too far down to be acceptable or comfortable. She was shocked, but didn't say anything.

She went home and told her parents and her father said he would shoot him. He went to the school, but Shelley was not sure whether he took his gun. He did, however, tell Pollard not to put his hands on his kids again. Shelley thinks her parents also spoke to the school inspector.

Very soon after that, Pollard left the school—fired, Shelley thinks—and another teacher, Mrs. Elliott, came to finish the year. The following school year, beginning in September 1966, Leskard school was closed and the children were bused to other country schools until the new Kirby Regional School opened.

The Teacher was not hired to teach at the new Kirby Regional School. In September 1967, when the new Kirby school opened, my mother told me the Teacher had gone to another school—miles away near Orillia. Someone else said he taught at a boys' school in Courtice. In less than two years, he returned to our area to live, and never taught again. Was never back in a classroom. Rumours followed him. Many thought he had lost his teaching licence, but a quick search on the Ontario College of Teachers website lists him as "inactive/non-practicing," not removed from the list, to this day.

To satisfy my curiosity as to what had happened, I phoned the woman who'd been the secretary at the new Kirby regional school. She hadn't known the Teacher, so had no idea why he was not hired.

"Was he near to retirement?" she asked me.

"No, he was still pretty young—maybe in his thirties."

She didn't know.

The Teacher returned to Clarke Township in about 1969 and lived in Orono with his parents after they sold the family farm. They were in a brick house on Bradley Street. One of Leskard's former students I spoke with had lived across the street from them in Orono. He too had heard that the Teacher had been fired from Leskard School and then from an Orillia school.

Soon after, the Teacher bought a lot immediately west of where I grew up on the eighth line of Clarke Township, and put a trailer on it. Young women were seen coming and going from the trailer and the rumours said he was paying them. My brother confirmed that Pollard did own the lot and the trailer, but didn't know about the other rumours. What bothers me now is that he might have been in that trailer—only a stone's throw away—when I visited Mom and Dad during my university years and after—and no one told me.

The Teacher's two aunts lived on Centre Street in Orono. Speculation by someone who knew him well was that he was "biding his time," waiting to inherit their money. After his parents were both gone, he rented a house in the south part of Orono and drank a forty-ouncer of rye every day. In an interview, I was told that the local doctor would get him to dry out every few months, but then he would go right back to drinking.

The Teacher bought a service station complete with snack bar, long gone now, on the east side of the 115 Highway across from Noon's Restaurant, now a Tim Hortons. He hired young girls, some as young as thirteen or fourteen, to help out at the snack bar. When he tried to kiss one of them, she slapped him. Guys that hung out at the station said he also made obscene comments to these girls while they worked.

"You know if you let a boy near your hoohoo you may end up having a puppy!" Pollard would laugh uproariously at his own jokes while the girls blushed with embarrassment.

A couple of the Teacher's former students—Ronnie (one of the Leskard school bullies), and Ricky Anderson (who had been in the same class as me)—seemed to be his friends. He was also friends with an old man who lived alone up the hill from the village. The Teacher would show up on a Saturday night with a case of twenty-four, drink twenty-two of them, go out to relieve himself, and then drive home drunk.

Chapter 30
University And Marriage

While preparing to go to university in the fall of 1967, I said to my mother, "Can we sit down and have a talk about sex? I'd rather learn from you than from someone else."

I'd only had the Family Encyclopedia and high school health class for information, and Nana, my mother's mother, who told me, "Sex is terrible, but if you have a good man, it won't be too bad."

I seldom dated until I met Grant in grade thirteen, and was not tempted to have sex. Some hugs and a few rushed kisses before I hopped out of the car after high school dances were all the experience I'd had. I guess my mother's frequent warnings about the back seats of cars was enough to keep me chaste. But I'd read *Wuthering Heights* and *Gone with the Wind*, so I knew passion must be out there somewhere—and I wanted to be prepared.

At my question, Mom looked at me and said, "There are some things I think you're still too young to know." I was eighteen. Leaving home. She walked away.

Mom and Dad had different reactions to me leaving for university. When I was packing, Dad peeked briefly into my room and then walked down the hall to my parents' bedroom. I could hear him crying, but I had little empathy—I just desperately wanted out, to escape the oppression and hypocrisy. My mother, on the other hand, helped me pick out new shoes and material I sewed into dresses and skirts to take with me, still following her old belief that everything is solved by new outfits.

In the weeks before I left, I found some of Dad's old university English textbooks in a cupboard Mom used. She'd been studying them. She was intelligent enough to go back to school, finish high school, and get a degree, but she never tried. When I came home the first time after beginning my classes, Dad's university books had disappeared, returned to the boxes where Mom had found them.

In my mind's eye, I can see my mother—her denial of responsibility for leaving us with the Teacher, the numbing of her emotions, her escape into ineffective ways of coping with her problems—and, by doing so, I see my own reactions. Years and years later, she said to me about the Teacher, "I didn't think that bothered you," and I realized that I felt the same toward her—I didn't think the distance I put between myself and her bothered her.

* * *

In 1967, when I was eighteen, I left for Trent University in Peterborough. When I started university, I tried to "fit in," but didn't have the social skills that others my age had, and in fact was an unformed, immature husk of a person needing to grow up. I hadn't been allowed to go out and experience things like other teens, so with the freedom I had at university, I drank, smoked, went out with the "wrong" guys, some older and more experienced than I was, disappeared to take long walks—like Dad—and thought about suicide—but I managed to do moderately well academically in my first year.

During my second year, night after night, I got up at three or four in the morning, awakened by terrifying dreams of toilets overflowing with waste. I'd pace the halls of the residence, frightened to go back to my room. I couldn't concentrate in class and, for the first time, fell behind with my assignments. I went to the university counselling service, sobbing, terrified about what was happening to me. I was so distraught the doctor prescribed strong medication. I stopped taking the pills after a week, because, on them, I couldn't function—sleeping fourteen hours a day and hardly awake the rest of the time.

Mother and Dad took me to their family doctor who sent me for a barium enema to see what my gut told him. In the end, I think everyone believed I had a predisposition for my Dad's "nervous condition," despite not knowing about inherited trauma or epigenetics. And that might have been partially true.

However, in addition, the psychological consequences of child sexual abuse have now been documented and include fear, anxiety, guilt, denial, confusion, withdrawal, and grief, among others (Gurnon 2016). In the article "A Monster in the Classroom" (Macleans, Nov. 2022), Mouallem makes the point that "Victims don't have the luxury of forgetting. Their abuser loomed, (as mine did), as they pursued careers... and... struggled with relationships. He loomed as they battled... PTSD, suicidal thoughts, panic attacks, self-harm, and substance abuse."

Over the years, I developed many of these same issues but they weren't seen for what they were. No one—not me, not my parents, not the doctor, or the university counsellors—connected my breakdown with my parents' restrictions, their unhappiness, Dad's drinking, Mom's pill taking, the Teacher, child molestation, or the decision to leave me in our village school.

I was willing to be labelled the "sick one," and tried to deal with my own sense of failure and shame rather than imply that my parents had issues of their own or that the Teacher had been a problem.

* * *

From the time I began university, I avoided going home. When summer vacation arrived, I lived with my aunt and uncle in Scarborough, and got a summer job there. My mother's sister chided me for not meeting young men my age and going out—the exact opposite of my mother. I couldn't win! But it was easier dealing with my aunt and uncle than my parents.

The summer between my second and third year of university, I met Joe, who became my first husband. He seemed like a dream come true to me, an escape. He lived in Toronto, was working, and shared a flat with other young men. Though there were warning signs about him, I dismissed them. By this time in my life, I'd been so controlled by my parents, I just wanted to live what I thought would be my own life, though still plagued by anxiety.

While working at a summer job in Scarborough, I had a severe panic attack. The human resources person recognized it for what it was and called an ambulance. I was rushed to the hospital emergency room, sobbing and shaking, but the doctors who saw me seemed impatient with me and my symptoms. I walked back to Joe's apartment, mystified as to what had happened to me.

Another day, while I was shopping in the local food mart, the cans on the shelves seemed to take on a life of their own and become blurry, until I had to sit down in the aisle, panting, and feeling as though I couldn't breathe. I waited until I could get up and walk out the door, without my groceries.

When Joe and I took a trip to Niagara Falls, I stopped along a path and broke into tears—but didn't know why. I felt as though I was becoming unglued. Throughout that summer, I continued to have more panic attacks.

When I looked up information on such attacks, I learned that the general consensus is you don't get over them on your own, but that didn't happen to me. The panic attacks stopped and I carried on with my life as though they hadn't happened.

Chapter 31
Parents And Families

Joe and I became engaged and, a few months after I graduated with my bachelor's degree, were married. Mom did try to warn me about him, I'll give her that, but by that time, I didn't trust her. And of course, her warnings were convoluted—things like "Women shouldn't marry anyone who is not as smart as they are." Did she mean that Joe was not as intelligent as me? He *had* flunked out of two universities and was working as an assistant in a photography studio. But he always spoke as though he knew much more about life than I did—and perhaps he did.

When I contemplated marriage, I wasn't judging my new husband's character. Instead I felt the same desire for escape as I had when I first started high school, and then again when I left home to go to university. To me, marriage *was* an escape. And, finally, I'd be living in Toronto. Looking back now, I can see that these were not good reasons to get married.

It wasn't until I married Joe that my mother described in detail one of her methods for dealing with her unhappiness with my father.

"If Joe upsets you, don't make a fuss. Go out and buy yourself something nice. Hide it in the back of the closet or in a drawer, and after a couple of months, bring it out and wear it. If Joe asks if it's new, you can honestly say, 'No, I've had this for ages.'" Over the years, Mom amassed a large collection of shoes, bags, hats, and dresses—a lifetime of sorrows patched up with stylish purchases. I tried this method to deal with the hurt, frustration, and isolation I felt in my marriage to Joe—but only once. When I brought out a dress I'd bought weeks before and tried to pass it off as "this old thing?" it felt phoney and dishonest—as indeed it was. I never told my husband I'd tried to trick him. It felt wrong, and wouldn't lead to the kind of relationship I wanted.

Only years later did I discover that my husband Joe lied and manipulated as a regular part of how he dealt with me. I hadn't realized how far apart our values were—and how close his values were to those of my mother.

Feelings of fear, sadness, guilt, and shame were still a regular part of my life. I could be shopping, working, out with my husband, and suddenly I would be teary, have overwhelming feelings that seemed to come from nowhere. And I was angry—anger came over me that I didn't understand. Joe and I argued incessantly. When I went to my family doctor, he sent me to a psychiatrist who prescribed valium. Though different from phenobarbital, it was the same solution my mother was offered all those years before—take a drug to numb the feelings rather than solve the problems. I stopped taking it when I learned it was addictive.

I went back to my family doctor again to see if he could help me. He recommended that I listen to what my husband said to me. He suggested that perhaps Joe was goading me and, before I got angry at what he was saying, I should listen carefully to see if he was *trying* to make me angry. I took my doctor's advice, and found out he was right! I pointed all this out to Joe, but he didn't stop his mean comments, judgments, and insults, and I continued to feel hurt—and angry. Not surprisingly, I had no effective or healthy ways to deal with him.

In addition, my husband didn't know I carried a ghost with me wherever I went—I had frightening dreams in which my Teacher appeared. I knew then that I could leave the village physically, but the Teacher came along with me no matter where I was.

* * *

I enrolled in Toronto Teachers' College, met new friends, graduated, began teaching and working toward a permanent teaching certificate. I loved teaching and discovered I was good at it.

We bought a house built in 1913 in the Beach area of Toronto, within walking distance of Lake Ontario. Over the next four years, I poured love into our new home—planted a wild flower garden, and built a rockery with chunks of granite from the walls of the old barn on my parents' property. We had limited money so did much of the remodelling on the house ourselves. We installed a new bathroom and kitchen, using marble from yard sales, blue and white tiles, and blue wallpaper. In addition, we fitted an elaborate antique fireplace into the living room, bought when a mansion in the town of Bowmanville was torn down, and collected old furniture at country auctions to complement our house.

In the meantime, Joe was let go from the photographer's assistant job he loved. He tried working for another photographer for a short time, quit, and then took a job with the Toronto Transit Commission in the photography department. I spent each evening, before I did

216

my class preparations, listening to him complain about his co-workers.

"They've never studied photography."

"They were moved from other departments in the transit department to take a few snaps of the buses and streetcars."

"They've never worked in a professional photo studio."

Joe was unhappy and unfulfilled. He felt he was more knowledgeable and experienced than his co-workers. I decided that listening to all this was part of my role as his wife, but it did take up a lot of my time—time I needed to plan my classwork.

In 1975, I was expecting our first baby. We went to Lamaze classes to prepare for the birth. I sewed a layette—flannelette onesies, hooded blankets, all in unisex colours. Our son was born a beautiful, healthy, impossibly cute baby. Though I still needed to teach part-time to supplement our income, I thought, finally, I had the life I really wanted. I was leaving behind the feelings of anxiety and inadequacy I had been living with since childhood. But it seemed the happier I became, the more miserable Joe was.

In 1976, the summer our son was a baby, Joe's father came from Calgary to visit. Suddenly, Joe wanted to move to Calgary, two thousand, three hundred miles away, start a photography business there, and live close to his parents. For months, I resisted and we argued. I had no reason to move. But then one day, he said, "Well, if you won't move, I'll go without you"—without us, me and our son.

I should have realized then that if Joe was willing to move away without us, our marriage was over, but I didn't have the courage to stand up for what I wanted. We sold our home, packed, and moved to Calgary, a city where I knew no one except my in-laws. While we drove west, I cried across every mile of the prairie. After we arrived, Joe's parents wanted us to live with them, but I had had my own home, my own privacy, and insisted we rent our own place. My permanent Ontario teaching certificate was no longer valid because education is regulated province-to-province so I thought perhaps this was the time to have a second baby. In 1978, we had our second son.

Joe spent all his time building his photography business, meeting new friends—and partying. He "lost" his wedding ring. While he became more and more distant, more critical, insulting, and dismissive of me, I sat alone at home night after night with two babies. Despite me moving out west with him, he had left us anyway.

* * *

Mom came to visit me in Calgary and Dad stayed home—not unusual because he refused to fly. She made several phone calls back home to see how he was and repeatedly got no answer. Finally, Dad phoned. Much later, through my mother, my dad, my brother, and my nana, I pieced together what had happened.

Dad had been drinking steadily since Mom had left to visit me. Two neighbours, regular drinking buddies, knew he was drinking far too much. He was so sick they took him to the hospital in Oshawa. One of those neighbours phoned my brother and said, "Get all the guns out of the house before your Dad comes home." There was an addiction treatment centre in Oshawa where he went after being discharged from the hospital. The twenty-eight-day programme started the journey that turned my father's addictive life around.

He didn't want my sister and me to know, but he phoned Mom while she was with me in Calgary to tell her where he was. My mother told me Dad thought none of us knew about his boozing, the drunk driving, his drunken stupors as he stumbled to bed each Saturday evening.

After Dad dried out, he joined AA. He still had a few years left before he would be able to retire from GM and knew he needed to clean up his act if he was going to receive his full pension. Perhaps that had been another factor that enabled him to stick with the AA programme. He took early retirement at age fifty-seven, two years after he quit the booze, but his journey back to wholeness began the night he was rushed to the hospital.

When he retired, gone were the shifts of work in a factory he hated—two weeks' nights, two weeks' days. Instead, he filled his time with things he loved—writing a column on song birds for the local newspaper, building bluebird boxes to nail onto fence posts around the township to encourage the return of the vanishing Eastern Bluebird, teaching school children to build bluebird boxes, taking courses in Canadian history, and volunteering with the local fair board and the historical society. To this day, when I'm home, I still see his bluebird boxes nailed to the tops of fence posts. He made new friends through AA and helped others kick their addiction to alcohol.

My mother joined Al-Anon (AA's companion group for family members) for a couple of meetings and then stopped going. She said that too many who attended smoked, but also, she felt that it was Dad who had the problem, not her.

* * *

A couple of years after I moved to Calgary, I went back to work—this time in an oil company, because I could leave at the end of the day and have the evening with my family—very different from when I was teaching. My marriage to Joe didn't improve, but I was getting out and meeting people. After another two years, a short attempt at marriage counselling, and many arguments that went nowhere, our marriage ended with him punching me senseless. I got no child support and Joe showed little interest in our sons. I was devastated.

As when I was eight years old, my world completely changed—and not due to my own choice. In four short years, I had gone from Toronto, a city I loved, to Calgary, a city I had never wanted to live in, with a completely different culture, gone from being a homeowner to losing our newly-bought home because, even though I had a job, I was not making enough money to pay the mortgage by myself, and I was on my own with two small children. If Mom and Dad had offered to take me and my boys in I would have moved back east, but they didn't.

I didn't realize at the time that everything I went through with Joe had left me traumatized. As when I was young and in Leskard school, I survived by being numb and in denial. I had no idea what I was feeling.

I struggled for a few years on my own and then married a second time.

Duncan was very different from Joe. He was intelligent, had an M.A. in psychology and a Ph.D. in management, was charismatic, loved opera and the theatre, and, if he hadn't been such an angry man, would have been a perfect companion. He was abusive but in a different way to Joe—his anger was out in the open—yelling and screaming in public and at home. I struggled every day to keep arguments with Duncan to a minimum and usually didn't succeed. I felt that I was responsible for him, as I had been responsible for my own safety in Leskard school.

Only through research into the long-term effects of childhood trauma have I discovered that having relationships with abusers as an adult is a common problem of those who have gone through what I did as a child. (Gurnon 2016). Duncan introduced me to psychology, which, like teaching, I was good at. He encouraged me to go to graduate school and become a clinical psychologist. In addition, Duncan and I started a successful consulting business, so my income was dependent on our partnership. However, though different in methodology, like Joe, Duncan was controlling and demanding. It didn't take long before he "ran the show." I built a well-constructed "false front" in order to cope, but had no idea who I was underneath my elegant designer dresses and full-length mink coat.

* * *

A few years after Dad stopped drinking, I flew back to Toronto to attend a conference. Mom and Dad came to meet me at my hotel on Avenue Road and we walked down the block to the Royal Ontario Museum to see an exhibit of wildlife photos. Dad knew the photographer and had even bought one of his limited edition prints of the Eastern Bluebird. After, we walked over to the campus of St Michael's College, part of the University of Toronto, once the home of St. Michael's college school that Dad and his brother had attended. He talked about his unhappiness when he was sent away from home to attend St. Mike's. He then turned to me and said he had heard the stories of abuse by priests at Catholic Schools, but, to his knowledge, nothing like that happened at St. Mike's, at least not when he was a student there. He made no reference to our village Teacher and the abuse that had occurred, and I said nothing.

When we went for a meal in Chinatown, my parents chatted about what was happening for them. Years before, when my granny passed away, Dad had received an inheritance. With the money, Mom and Dad re-did the house—put on new siding, a new roof, and an extension for a TV room. They had a pool installed. It was mainly Mom who used the pool because of her love of swimming. While we ate, Mom talked about how they needed to either buy a new liner for the pool or get it filled in—but Dad wanted a new pickup truck instead.

When Mom went to the washroom, Dad said, "I have the right to say how we spend the money. I worked. I earned it." Though sober, Dad had maintained his arrogance and misogyny and still lived his life as though he was the only one with hopes and dreams.

I said, "You never let Mom work, so she couldn't earn her own money." My mother was caught in a Catch-22.

He still insisted he was right. After my brother, sister, and I left home to marry and start our own families, my mother was the last person left in the house with Dad—the last one he could control—and he needed that last vestige of power. As my mother once said to my brother, "With your dad, it's his way or the highway."

The pool was filled in and Dad bought the truck he wanted. In less than two years he died of complications from smoking, and Mom sold the truck. The pool stayed filled in.

* * *

I "woke up" in the last year of my second marriage, began to fight back and tell my truth. In 1998, I went to therapy and told my psychologist I wanted my life back. On the way to a divorce, Duncan died in July 1999, of cancer.

Dad's life began when he stopped drinking, mine with my husband's death. I became aware of what I'd done to let others control me. After four and a half years on my own, I met and married Bill, who wanted to accompany me in facing truth in our lives.

After both Mom and Dad had passed away, I started my journey back in time, to the school, the Teacher, and the village where I grew up—the journey to lift the cloud of despair that had prevented me from living a full life.

Chapter 32
The Last Years Of The Teacher

When I contacted Brian Buckley through Facebook to ask for his memories of the Teacher, he wrote to me of incidents that had happened in and near Orono of which I was previously unaware.

Brian hadn't seen the Teacher for a few years when he'd stopped in at a service station up the highway to get a fill up. A man came out to put the gas in the tank and Brian recognized Ronnie, who'd been a few years ahead of him in elementary school. When Brian went into the station to pay for the gas, he could see into a back room, where playing cards lay spread out on the table.

The Teacher was pouring a drink into a plastic cup from a forty-ouncer. He put down the bottle, lifted the cup to his lips, closed his eyes, and downed the whole thing. He turned to the table to pick up his cards, and asked Ronnie to bring him a bag of chips when he was finished with that sale—one of the big bags, and some KitKats. He added that he hadn't had anything to eat since breakfast.

Ronnie took Brian's money and looked at him as he put it into the cash register and handed him the receipt. "Do I know you?" he said.

Brian could have said, "Yes," but he didn't want to. Better to let it rest.

He looked past him again at the Teacher and recalled the stories he'd heard about him. How his uncle had said the Teacher wasn't physically normal for a man. How grown women shunned him after being set up on dates with him.

He told me he wondered, maybe they were only rumours, but maybe that's why he liked little girls.

* * *

Another day, Brian parked the car in Orono and he and his wife Carol got out on the main street to do some shopping. They headed to the convenience store on the corner to pick up milk and butter. Just as they climbed the cement steps from the road up to the sidewalk, a man came out of the shop door.

"Here, let me get that door for you," he said to Carol, not too clearly, sort of mumbling, half slurring the words. As he attempted a sweeping grand gesture bow, he stumbled.

Brian glanced down at the man's trousers and saw a spreading dark stain. A pool of urine formed on the sidewalk. The man looked up with jaundiced eyes. Even from several feet away, he smelled of alcohol and as though he hadn't bathed in weeks. He teetered, leaned precariously, trying to catch himself. As though in slow motion, he fell on his side half-way down the steps, his legs sprawled apart, his arms flailing for a hand hold.

It took a few seconds for Brian to realize he knew the man. He saw the bald head and heard the familiar voice demanding help. It was the Teacher, laid out over three steps, in front of him and his wife. They held their breath as they got on either side of him, took his arms and pulled him upright.

"I'm sorry... so sorry. Thank you so much... helping me." He looked closely into Brian's face. "Do you know me?"

Brian looked to Carol, and mouthed the words, "Let's leave him here. Just leave him." He climbed the rest of the way back up to the door of the convenience store.

The Teacher was stumbling now—holding himself bent over at the waist so he could lurch from the hood of one parked car to the trunk of the next as he fumbled his way down the main street of town. But then he stopped, looked back at Brian as though a part of his brain had just lit up. He yelled, "I KNOW you. I taught you. I TOLD you, you would never amount to anything!"

Brian wondered how the Teacher was going to get home, or back up the highway. Surely, he wouldn't attempt to drive. It was the last he ever saw of him.

* * *

When I spoke with Cathy Spry via Facebook chat, I learned what had happened to her after leaving Leskard school. She and her parents moved to Maple Grove where she went to elementary school, and after, she attended Bowmanville High School, before training and qualifying as a nurse. She and her high school sweetheart married and started a family. She stretched out her maternity leave as long as she could to be with her children while they were toddlers, then, in 1983, headed back to work at the large regional hospital in Bowmanville.

One of the first things she noticed was a piano in the patients' lounge. Her nursing supervisor said, "It was a gift from a patient who died just a couple of weeks ago."

"Oh, really? That was generous."

"Yes, I don't think he had many family members to leave it to. He was a teacher a long time ago. Out in a country village. I guess he loved music."

Cathy thought, *No, it couldn't be. No way.* But she couldn't stop herself from asking what his name was.

When the other nurse told her, she told me she went hot and cold in quick succession. She burst out, "That piano, that man who died, the Teacher... he molested most of the little girls in our school. He molested me."

"Oh my god, that's horrible. Oh, Cathy, I'm so sorry. Of course, we didn't know, and even if we had, we had to treat him the same as all the other patients."

"Yes, of course," Cathy said, and left to begin her duties.

Later, on her break, she heard about the Teacher from other nurses.

"It was horrible. I never had to nurse a patient like that before."

"Why?" Cathy asked, "What did he have?"

"Cirrhosis. He was swollen—his legs and stomach. The legs were purple and huge, the skin shiny and stretched—really ghastly. He couldn't stop itching."

"Don't forget the bedsores," added another nurse. "I've never seen any as bad as that. He needed to be turned every hour, and even that didn't really help."

"And the smell—it was unbearable. He vomited a lot. I had to clean him up more than once."

Jill had told me she and her family visited the Teacher in the hospital but even they didn't want to stay too long. A nurse said when one of the relatives left the Teacher's room, she looked as though she was going to pass out.

Cathy said she didn't want to revel in another's misery but she had breathed a sigh of relief that his downfall was alcohol, not the misery of more little girls.

* * *

As Cathy contemplated what she'd been told, the head nurse, Mrs. Bernston, came up to her, "I just want you to know that the rumour about my husband beating Billy Churchill was not true."

Wow, Cathy thought, that certainly came out of nowhere. Mrs. Bernston beat a hasty retreat after the statement of her husband's innocence—but why? Cathy wondered what she hoped to gain after all these years. Was she trying to rescue his reputation at this late date? Cathy pondered all this as she went back to work.

* * *

The Teacher's obituary in the *Orono Times* read as follows:

Pollard—Jim. Suddenly at Orono on January 22, 1983. James Pollard aged 51 years. Son of the late George and Laura Pollard. Rested at the Barlow Funeral Home, Orono. Service was held at the Lang Chapel on Monday at 2:00 P.M. Spring Internment Orono Cemetery.

Except he hadn't died in Orono, nor had he died suddenly. It was a slow, prolonged death. There was nothing in the obituary about him having been a teacher and principal in a country school. Nothing of his love of music or the harm he had done. Perhaps the person who wrote the obituary didn't even know him, or didn't want to tell the truth about him in death, as no one had in life.

Chapter 33
I Return To The School:

In June 2018, I left my car at the village church where I was staying, and walked up the hill—that hill I'd raced up so many times when I was late for school. I turned into the old school yard and looked to the right to see the former baseball diamond, now grass-covered, and two new maple trees—they must have been planted some years ago from the size of the trees. Further to the right, I saw the huge maple trees that had been there when I'd attended school here— trees that had been lined up for well over seventy years along the side of the old baseball diamond, at the top of our toboggan hill. What had seemed like a huge area when I was young was now a generous front lawn. Then I looked straight ahead at the old village school—built nearly one hundred and fifty years before. Five years after I finished grade eight and went to high school, this rural school was closed and sold to a new owner who'd turned it into a home. I hadn't entered the school since I was fourteen—fifty-five years before.

The front of the school had changed little in the years since I was young. Two storeys, white clapboard with a peaked roof, a bell tower on the peak, and two doors on the front—one for the girls on the right, one for the boys on the left. I walked up two steps onto the cement slab that fronted the building, and wondered if this was the original cement where we had skipped double-dutch. Was some of the chalk dust from our hopscotch still deep in its cracks? I remembered the many times we also drew hopscotch outlines on the dirt just off the cement slab, but tried not to remember the times the Teacher turned the rope while we skipped.

I went up to the door, knocked...waited...knocked again. Anna, a woman in her fifties, came to the door. Her hair was tousled and she wore a t-shirt and jeans. She looked at me blankly—she'd forgotten I'd planned to come over that day. She was busy cleaning so she and her husband could get the house ready to sell in preparation for moving west. But she invited me in.

I entered a small boot room built onto the front of the school, then turned left and walked through the "girls' door." Anna pointed out that, to the left of the door, the original stairs leading to the upper floor of the school were still there, unchanged. Straight in front, the next door led into what had been the girls' cloakroom, where we'd hung our coats on hooks on the wall. To the left, the former girls' washroom was now a modern bathroom with a shower. Straight ahead was the door into the classroom where I'd spent five years. As I walked across the threshold, I could feel my chest tighten. A shakiness ran through my body.

I looked around and tried to imagine the classroom as I'd known it so many years before—the rows of desks, the children at work. The windows were the same—large, almost to the ceiling—the sills above where our heads would be bent over our desks so we couldn't look out and be distracted by nature. Then, the window sills held souvenirs from our nature hikes, like stones, bits of bark and the cecropia moth we'd imprisoned in a large pickle jar.

The blackboards that had covered the entire front of the classroom, behind the Teacher's desk, had been replaced with faux wood paneling and a floor-to-ceiling stone backdrop to a wood stove. To the right, a long kitchen counter stood in front of a parallel counter with a stove, sink, and refrigerator. The front corner of the classroom where the Teacher had played the piano all those years ago, was empty. I took several deep breaths to calm my tension.

The same support pillars held up the ceiling. Beside one of them, there'd been a large heat register where we'd placed our wet mitts and boots to dry in the winter. Inevitably, they got wet again at the next recess or lunch hour, but we always hoped they would be a bit drier or at least warm. I mentioned a few of these things to Anna, the owner of the school, and she began to tell me what she knew, derived from the book, *Out of the Mists*, written many years ago by local historian, Helen Schmidt, and my former high school Vice-Principal, Sid Rutherford. The same book I had a copy of at home. Anna asked if I wanted to see the upstairs, though she said it was much different from the original.

"Years ago," she said, "my husband and I heard a knock on the door. A woman stood there, pointing to our roof. She'd seen a fire when she drove by, so she stopped to tell us."

I'd heard this story from my parents who had lived out their lives in my childhood home, west of the village.

As Anna and I walked up the polished wooden stairs, she explained, "That fire destroyed the roof and much of the upper floor, so it all had to be replaced."

"You were very lucky you were warned," I said

"Actually, it was quite mysterious, because we didn't know the woman, and never saw her again."

The upper floor was indeed very different from the single open classroom when my brother, sister, and I attended the school. Now it was divided into bedrooms opening off a hallway. I looked to see if the old windows and storage room were still there. The windows were—or at least replicas of the originals—the storeroom was not. I recalled the many Christmas concerts and Red Cross meetings held in the upper classroom. Anna and I went out onto the upstairs balcony where she invited me to sit while she got out her notes.

"I have wonderful memories of visiting my father in this old school house after he bought it in the 1967 auction," Anna said. Afterwards, she and her husband bought the house from him and raised their children here.

"The school is representative of old values and a simpler time," she said, as though she knew the history of the school, the students, and their stories. I bristled at the description—I wanted to interject, "You don't know. This was my school. "

She continued, "People came to visit the school during a recent township 'Open House of Historic Buildings,' who told stories of sliding down the hill on toboggans. One girl was taught to skate by another child."

I replied, "Yes, I remember tobogganing and skating here. The school was good for some children."

She looked at me, catching the tone of my voice that indicated I was not including myself, and said, "You are the only person who has indicated they didn't have a good time at this school."

Anna's young daughter had said to her many times that she wished she had lived back then and gone to the school in those "simpler times," that to her represented "old values."

I remarked, "Those times were good for some, but not good for everyone. Some children came to school hungry and had little or nothing to eat for lunch."

I had just wanted to see and experience the school again. I hadn't intended to tell this woman what I'd endured at the school, but again and again she referred to people who said they'd enjoyed their time at the school. I repeated that not all people's experience of the school was the same, but I could see the doubt in her eyes as she got a file of notes that had been tucked into her local history book. She looked down at the book and then up at me.

I said, thinking I was on safe ground, "By the time I came to this school, the upstairs was the junior classroom."

She flipped through her history-of-the-area book. "The upstairs room was a meeting room and a club room. Dances were held here."

"In the early days, yes, but later it was the classroom for the younger children."

"When we had the open house, someone came whose grandfather played the fiddle for the dances."

"Yes, that's likely true," I said, not really sure, but I too had read that the original use of the upper room *was* as a community space. "But from 1957, and possibly a couple of years before, it was the junior classroom."

She paused and returned to, "You are the only one who has ever said that their time at the village school wasn't happy."

"There was a teacher who was a problem."

"Why, what was the issue?"

"He was a pedophile."

She looked startled, "Oh, that's so sad," then paused and said, "I really wish I didn't know." This was clearly a shock to her, a surprise she didn't have time to process at the moment.

"Were children molested upstairs?"

I was surprised at her question—and felt shame at the memory. Had she known I'd been abused upstairs? No, she couldn't possibly know about me, but maybe she'd heard stories.

"Yes, it happened upstairs, but he did it downstairs, too." I didn't tell her about me.

I said goodbye and walked out of the school, upset that I'd revealed to a stranger something that had haunted my whole life. Tension, guilt, that twisted-gut feeling that it was my job to keep the tawdry past secret, rushed at me.

All I'd feared had come out in that woman's response, "You are the only one who said their time in the village school was bad or difficult." *You are the only one.*

Later that day, I received an email from Anna, reminding me that she and her husband didn't want me using any photos I'd taken as it is not a school any longer, but a private home. I feared she was angry with me that the past had been brought to her attention. She wanted to think a certain thing about the school—"a simpler time"—and I'd blown a hole in that. But possibly I was too quick to judge someone who had no idea of the history of the school?

Opening wounds, even ones that hadn't directly impacted the people who lived in the school now, was clearly uncomfortable.

Chapter 34
Final Thoughts

When I moved from Courtice to Leskard in 1957, my life changed trajectory from what it could have been. Instead of the confident, happy young girl I was at eight years of age, I acknowledge that I will never fully recover that confidence. For years, I fought anxiety, depression, feelings of failure, unhappy memories, and a deep numbness inside me, only to realize that those feelings have now become part of my identity.

After all the conversations, online interviews, library and museum research looking for explanations, had I found what I was looking for? I did find some answers to the questions, "Why was a pedophile allowed to teach in my school?" "Why didn't anyone do anything about it?" and, "Who let it happen?" I had originally set out to research *other* families and had come to the realization that I had to write about *my own* parents and family as well as others. With every sandwich my mother made and sent to school for class parties, she implied that what was happening was all right with her.

My parents could have looked at alternative schools for us, and possibly they did, though I was never told that. They could have asked our parish priest for help. Did they tell my Nana or Granny about the problem? My aunt, my father's sister, said that likely Granny, their mother, never knew about the Teacher, or she would have insisted her favourite granddaughter, oldest child of her oldest son, be taken out of the village school. Also, knowing how my Nana responded when her boarder molested my brother, I am sure she would have urged—no, insisted—that we be taken out of the school. I believe now that my parents would have had support in finding another school, but possibly they were both too proud and overly sensitive to implied criticism to ask for help.

There were many reasons families didn't act when someone threatened their children. Some families were broken. Too broken to deal with a big issue like pedophilia. Our family looked fine from the outside, but, with Dad's alcoholism and anxiety, Mom's reliance on strong medication, and their general unhappiness, we seemed broken to me. The Gregorys struggled to make ends meet. Jill's family didn't see the problems staring them right in the face—both their attitudes, and the fact they were related to the Teacher led them to protect him rather than their daughter, even in the face of serious crime. Other village families were overburdened and overwhelmed—some lived on the edge of poverty, some dealt with domestic abuse, health issues, or simply the struggle of putting food on the table. Anger reigned in some families that had been broken by the effects of the Second World War, and in the Smith and Bernston families whose fathers were angry for reasons unknown to me.

Some families were not affected directly by the Teacher—their children weren't involved, like those of Reverend Long who lived in Orono, and Earl and Mona McDonald, the store keepers. The Teacher didn't molest boys—though there were rumours to the contrary—so families with boys were not directly involved, though their sons witnessed some of the abuse. Some girls were too old by the time he started teaching to be of interest to him, and some he just left alone—perhaps he was just not attracted to them in that way.

Some people were just too timid to deal with major issues or authority figures like those in a school. "Respect your betters" was still part of the culture.

Some families outside the immediate area knew about the Teacher but felt it was up to those who lived in Leskard to deal with him. If no one did, well then, that was it—case closed. And there was a belief in magical thinking—if there really *had* been an issue, *someone* would have done something.

Because of all this, the Teacher was able to carry on as he pleased—as one writer put it, he was "able to maintain a lifestyle that violated the social norms and laws ..." (Kristjanson 2013)

* * *

My hunger for information on rural culture led me to read *Paradise: Class, Commuters, and Ethnicity in Rural Ontario,* in which the author Stanley Barratt quoted a Protestant minister who had served in Mono Township, northwest of Toronto. He stated that among the distraught elderly women who came to him for comfort and guidance, the root problem for a high proportion of them was the same: either they had been victims of physical abuse as children, or they had been victims of incest. The minister commented, "What was most remarkable was that the memories of such physical abuse and incest remained alive in the minds of these women sixty and seventy years later, to the extent of reducing their capacity to cope."

The women who'd come to the luncheon in the Leskard village church who raised their hands to say, "Me, too," had not forgotten. Women I interviewed later had not forgotten. I had not forgotten. I had to assume that men who had hung around with the Teacher as young men had not forgotten either—and, indeed, some hadn't.

Anne Petrie, in her book *Gone to an Aunt's* (1998), wrote about the attitudes toward sex in the fifties and sixties. "Most parents—that is, most mothers—were usually too embarrassed to talk to their children about sex."

And in the case of child sexual abuse, the focus of my mother seemed to be on the "sexual" aspect of what had happened in our school, rather than the "abuse" part. So, the whole topic was taboo.

Memory is a tricky thing. It is fluid, particularly memories from childhood. People saw things, heard things, and gossiped among themselves. Recollections were distorted. I pondered all this as I thought about what villagers and former classmates had revealed to me. This was hard stuff. It was difficult for me but also for others, like the junior teacher who had heard rumours at the time but was unable, due to the school system and the laws in the fifties, to do anything.

Local men, as adults, had hung around with someone who had preyed on young girls. Perhaps some had since reflected and saw their behaviour back then as inadequate— hanging around with a man they knew was a drunk and a child molester. But, if so, were their self-judgments fair? Did they feel shame and embarrassment that, over sixty years ago, nothing was done? Were their actions back then reflective of the time? Or reflective of how rural communities handled such issues? Now we have a different understanding and awareness of coercive power, manipulation, the vulnerability of children, and what to do when boundaries are crossed.

Did some responsibility have to be carried by everyone? Even me? I got away as quickly as I could, went to high school and university, then got married. I never talked with my parents about what had happened. Never got angry with them for making me go back to school after the Teacher had molested me. I just felt sickened when I thought of him. Afraid. Haunted. On the night of July third, 2018, just after I started this research, I dreamed I was hitting a fat-faced man, like the Teacher, over and over on the head with a heavy object the size of a brick.

I knew that going back in time to get explanations was never going to be an easy task. What I got was a series of stories—linked by a village and a man, the Teacher. Each person I spoke with added pieces to the story—told part of the truth or as much truth as they were able to remember, and were willing to talk about. I felt that bringing it all out into the open, speaking about it in a way that wasn't done all those years ago, was important. Though I still might end up with only part of the picture, it might be enough to be a relief for me.

Now there are so many things I would like to ask my parents about what happened in the village and the school when I was a child. In addition, I'd like to ask my father what role he played in the decision to leave my sister and me in the school. But they are both gone. I waited because that was the nature of the relationship we had. One in which there were taboos. Taboos against discussing the most important issues going on at the time. There were lines I was afraid to cross, even when I became an adult.

Neither of my parents ever asked me what my experience was like. It was as though by sending my sister and me back to the school, they had found a "solution" to the problem. Except for my mother telling me about what the Teacher was doing to other children and other families, my parents said little. Perhaps they lacked the imagination it would have taken to see how, even being taught by the Teacher, being in the same room with him year after year, was traumatizing.

My parents never meant to be neglectful parents—we always had food on the table and clothes to wear. They loved us in the best way they could. But neither of them had the ability to step outside their own issues to pay attention to the emotional needs of their children, and they created a family culture in which no one's needs were met.

* * *

If I'd tried to have the Teacher charged when I was in my twenties, he might have been found responsible for what he did—but it never occurred to me until much later, after he'd died. I felt guilty for not speaking up sooner, but I just wanted to get away and stay away from my parents and the village. In addition, I was suffering from nervousness and anxiety myself.

Despite dreaming of the Teacher while in my twenties, I never put him together with my emotional upsets. I'd learned to ignore, to avoid, and to endure lies. I was unable to recognize others' meanness or madness, and I minimized my own pain. I know now that traumatic memory can haunt not only the mind, but also the nervous system. And, when those memories are embedded in one's nervous system, they can leave a person hyper-vigilant, dissociative, or numb for years. The term for that now is post-traumatic stress syndrome, but in the 1950s and sixties, PTSD was a term reserved for war veterans, not young girls who had been touched and taught by a predator.

I was driven out of Leskard by memories of the monster that dwelt there and the lack of protection from him. I moved to Toronto first, then two thousand, three hundred miles away to Calgary. Even in Calgary, I kept moving, changing house seven times while my children were young—and then I moved to England. After that, I moved to Hawaii, then back to Nelson, British Columbia, and finally returned to Calgary to be near my sons and grandsons. I can see now that moving was an attempt to deal with my anxiety, though ineffectively.

* * *

We can never really know what went on in the Teacher's mind, but we can look at how he lived his life and finally died. After returning to the Leskard and Orono area in the late sixties after two years away, he lived thirteen more years before dying in the Bowmanville Hospital at age fifty-one. Young, but perhaps not for someone who drank himself to death. Cirrhosis, a degenerative disease, is the official name for what he died of—it is one of the fastest ways to shorten one's life—a form of suicide perhaps.

I never saw him after he ceased being a teacher, when he was drunk, owning a gas station, falling down in the middle of the street in Orono, dying, bloated, stinking, and ugly, dead, but every once in a while, the Teacher still felt alive to me. So, when my mother told me the Teacher had died, I gave a sharp intake of breath and said, "Thank god."

She looked startled, turned to me and uttered those unbelievably naive words, "I didn't think that bothered you."

Later, I sat and thought about the conversation I never had with my mother. I felt regret crush my chest—because I hadn't told her how it was for me. For my sister. But, I already knew what would happen if I approached the topic. She'd feel attacked, angry, maybe guilty. No, she'd cry, but she wouldn't have let herself feel guilty. I'd feel guilty.

The frustration was that now I knew two things. We would never have this conversation, and she would never have to face the reality of the position my sister and I had been put in.

* * *

I drove up the hill and parked my rented car on the road in front of my childhood home. When my mother died, my husband and I could have bought her house, this house I grew up in.

I pictured the polished pine floors upstairs and down— wide boards from ancient trees, cut in the lumber mill in the village. I could see in my mind's eye the large archway between the big kitchen where we ate, and the living room, the built-in glass-fronted cabinets and drawers in the living room and their counterpart on the other side of the stairwell, in the room we always called the dining room, but never ate in. I saw the windows on the main floor looking out onto the garden, my huge bedroom upstairs with the window looking out over the hills toward the village of Leskard, the bathroom my parents renovated but not to the point where anyone would call it the beautiful bathroom Mom wanted.

Ah, and my mother's endless collections! China eggs, large and small, fishing floats in all colours of glass sitting in a handmade basket, antique toys, glass paperweights she bought from antique auction sales, books in stacks, waiting to go back to the library in Oshawa. Dad always said, "Give your mother a surface and she'll decorate it!" I remembered the glass-fronted bookcase in the living room that had been Granny's, filled with a full original set of Foxfire including the Salt book, that Dad treasured, even though he was not a homesteader. He liked to think he was, hence the books.

I turned to look at the garden out front, the old twisted apple trees, the asparagus patch, the walnut trees that stood by the road, the spruce trees lining each side of the driveway. But the beauty became white and harsh and tragic when winter set in.

Though it was still summer, I could feel the dark encircle me, and a sense of doom move through me. I needed to be safe. When night falls in Calgary, I listen to music, put a log on the fire, read—but I wouldn't be able to do that here, where it had happened. Perhaps only a family from outside the area, that didn't know the history, could live in our old house—truly live—but now I need somewhere with no ghosts.

* * *

Some events in history are so huge, so horrifying, and leave so much damage, they are memorialized, but there is no plaque for us, no marker in our village that says what happened. Our school was small—with a maximum of thirty or forty students in total per year, half of them girls—not a huge number like the number of boys abused at the Bowmanville Training School.

A friend of the author Elizabeth Rosner (2017), said that "suffering doesn't really transform until there is an apology; the victims need to be heard by the perpetrators, but they also need to feel the atonement." In our case, there will never be an apology; never be reparation for what we went through. But, I have to believe that, by bringing this out into the light of day, we will be heard. The village children need to stop carrying the shame for what happened—the shame that the Teacher should have had.

It is almost unbelievable what one man can do to so many with just one hand on a leg, a thigh. The *sleight of hand* that can change a young girl for the rest of her life. This book was written to honour and memorialize all of us.

Chapter 35

Knowledge And Research Catch Up

What happened long ago in our village, at our school, was a textbook case of pedophilia—but in the fifties, the textbook had yet to be written. Research into the actions and characteristics of pedophiles and the effect on children who have been molested had yet to be done. Nevertheless, our situation ticked all the boxes.

When I went to elementary school in the 1950s, the sexual abuse of children was ubiquitous. My mother warned me about strangers, particularly about getting into cars with strangers. It was impossible not to know that adults might prey on youngsters—yet people commonly looked the other way. In 1953, Alfred Kinsey reported that "fully a quarter of all girls under the age of 14 reported that they had experienced some form of sexual abuse, including exhibitionism, fondling, or incest (rates roughly similar to those reported today). Yet, these findings evoked virtually no public interest." (Mintz, 2012).

Laws and attitudes toward child sexual abuse have changed substantially from the 1950s. A Canadian expert on the issue, William L. Marshall, quoted in Filteau 2004, said that "in the late 1960s there was so little professional literature available on people who sexually abuse minors that 'you could read it all in one morning.'" Marshall went on to state that in Canada and the U.S. and a few other countries around the world, there has been a sharp learning curve on sex abuse. Years ago, "pervasive societal, legal, professional and organizational obstacles made it far more difficult to recognize child sexual abuse, report it, prevent it, arrest or treat perpetrators of abuse." There were also gaps in the law, lax prosecution of offenders, societal attitudes that demeaned children's claims, and implicit anti-disclosure policies by organizations serving children—public schools and a wide range of non-profit religious and child-service organizations. (Filteau 2004) Such organizations tended to disbelieve claims by children and to stand by the adult who was accused, as happened in our village.

I have learned that, while the laws in the 1950s (Bala 1999) had an impact on what happened at our school, the decisions made, and what was done or not done, even more influential was the informal rural cultural attitude that a handful of powerful families could rule the community as if it were their own personal fiefdom (Barrett 1994)—as did the family of my Teacher. It was a persistent and narrow-minded view that outsiders like my family, who didn't adhere to this custom, were considered suspicious.

Over recent decades, there has been a much greater tendency to believe a child's report—and much more awareness of the impact or damage inflicted by sexual abuse. Only now are professionals in society really paying attention to the criminal nature of perpetrators' actions and the effect on those who have been victimized—and that, inadequately. An article written by Lowen (2019) in thoughtco.com, states that "child sexual abuse is" still a "significantly underreported crime that's difficult to prove or prosecute. Most perpetrators of child molestation, incest, and child rape are rarely identified or brought to justice." And that is in 2019!

Violence, especially against children, is difficult for many people to accept, acknowledge and face. If the truth is inconvenient, particularly if it involves family members or admired figures in the community (University of Michigan Science Daily, 2019), people simply won't believe it. That was true in our village. But in addition to disbelief, many people, like my parents, did know, but didn't act.

Denial is actually not knowing. If something is so heinous that we simply don't want to know, we will erase it from our conscious minds. Disavowal on the other hand, is knowing, but not acknowledging the effects of something (Kahn-Harris, K. 2018). My parents knew what had happened, and my mother spoke to me about the Teacher, so they were not in denial. Instead, they disavowed the effect of sending my sister and I to a school to be taught by a pedophile. Yes, they took us out of school for a few weeks, but when those in authority didn't fire the Teacher, and other parents sent their children back to school, or ignored the whole issue, they acquiesced.

You might think that if you showed someone the facts, they would adjust their views to fit what is actually real and provable, but, often, that is not true. People tend to dismiss facts that don't fit their ideological worldview (Bardon 2020), sometimes angrily. The commonly quoted statement by Philip A. Fisher is apt: "I have already made up my mind, don't confuse me with facts." People use motivated reasoning—their preferred conclusion—to decide what evidence to accept. In other words, "I already believe 'x' so I am going to defend that rather than admit I might be mistaken." (Bardon, 2020)

Today's laws reflect that, in Canada, the sexual abuse of children is wrong and illegal, but we humans have ways of prioritizing abuse—which abuse we see as worse than others.

Generally, touching a child inappropriately is not thought of as bad or serious as oral assault, penetration, or other kinds of assault. So possibly my parents thought that what the Teacher was doing was bad or wrong, but not as bad as it could have been, so a nine or ten-year-old should be able to deal with it. However, that doesn't explain the fact that they knew the Teacher was stalking one girl and, later, had heard the rumour that he had impregnated one of his students. I learned, through my many conversations with former classmates, that that rumour is still alive today—sixty years later.

* * *

Through my own experience, and in talking with others, I have discovered that the effect of one Teacher on the students and the village I lived in, has had far reaching consequences. Even the so-called "minor" abuse we experienced has caused long-term traumatic damage to some victims. Sixty years on, four of the former classmates I've been able to contact refused to talk about their experiences, as did I—until recently.

Research shows that pedophiles often seek out shy, handicapped, and withdrawn children, or those who come from troubled or underprivileged homes. Then they shower those children with attention, and/or gifts. Several of the people I interviewed mentioned that some girls received gifts from the Teacher, implying that they were benefiting from abuse and possibly "using" the Teacher. But those actions were all part of the grooming process—the grooming not only of the child, but of the parents, (naasca.org/2012) for a sexual goal.

Another complicating factor in finding out the truth of our village and the Teacher is that, in the 1940s and fifties, a common belief was that victims bring on their own victimization. This attitude reveals a lack of empathy for children who are victimized. The consequence of this is, if victims were believed to be at least partly to blame, then they were also responsible for keeping themselves safe—as the police and my parents' advice to "never be alone with the Teacher" implied.

This old attitude is *still* reflected in policing. Questions like "What were you wearing?" or "How much did you have to drink?" often face rape victims—implying their guilt rather than their victim status—and harken back to old attitudes that bad things only happen to you if you do something wrong. (Szalavitz, 2018) These attitudes and the response from police and the justice system, have led to a system that actually lets some sexual predators "off the hook."

According to my mother, a girl who dressed in what she considered a "provocative outfit" was "asking for it." Girls who drove in a car with a boy were putting themselves in his hands, so if he took advantage, the girl was at least partially responsible. "She was leading him on." "She should have known better." It was the girl's fault if she was molested, attacked, even raped. The responsibility to stay out of the hands of predators was hers—as it was ours at nine and ten years of age.

Caregivers' reluctance to confront behaviour that is questionable is another factor that helps predators victimize children. Amy Wright Glenn's article (2018) states, "Intuition is parents' greatest tool to fight child abuse—and many won't use it." She says that the feeling we often get that something is "just not right" is there for a reason (Gavin de Becker 1997), but we are taught from an early age to only pay attention to concrete information ("don't be silly") and often, in the case of child abusers, that information can be ambiguous. Some in our village didn't trust their own instincts about what was happening or what to do about it, or they were so uncomfortable with the whole situation, they "stuck their heads in the sand."

Many offenders will stop targeting a certain child if the parents speak up. Berkower (in Glenn 2018) found that "most offenders report 'their greatest fear' is having someone call them out on their grooming behaviour and this can be a 'huge deterrent.'" It is possible that I was never victimized in *exactly* the same way again by our Teacher because my parents did at least take us out of school for a period of weeks, trying to see if something would be done. However, that didn't stop him from speaking inappropriately with me or victimizing other girls.

Research into the characteristics of child molesters has provided a wealth of material on their thoughts, actions, and rationalization of their actions—information my parents didn't have sixty years ago. For example, many abusers are narcissists—i.e. interested in their own needs only and with a tendency to blame others—but they know they have to fit in with the rest of society, so they are "very adept at impression management—managing the ways others perceive them." (Arabi 2018) They often display charm, a handsome appearance, intellect, and social acumen. They are defended by cronies who claim the victims who speak out are the problem.

Pedophiles often demonstrate similar characteristics to each other, such as: being male, single, with few friends in their age group, often talking to or treating children like equals. They are fascinated with children and childhood activities—which explains the Teacher joining the girls at recess to skip rope, or organizing Red Rover. They have a specific age of child they target, and often their own environment or special room will be decorated in child-like décor (Montaldo, C. 2019), as was the Teacher's bedroom.

Pedophiles often prefer children close to puberty who are sexually innocent—our Teacher paid most attention to girls from age eight to ten or eleven. As in our case, it is common for the offender to be someone known to the child, such as a neighbour, coach, babysitter, or teacher.

The Sociopath Next Door, Stout (2006) states that when someone acts in an abusive manner to us, we project our own sense of morality, conscience, and empathy onto them. We excuse their behaviour as "misunderstandings" and minimize the damage done. We see that they are well-liked, so we feel we must be wrong. That leads us to ignore our gut instincts. And the sexual predator takes advantage of that.

Decades later, there has been a roll-out of victim services indicating an increasing concern for victims. There has been a cultural expansion of empathy and sensitivity to those experiencing harm and suffering. However, victims still fear blame and scrutiny, and often, they fear their abuser.

I did some online searching for information about what *is* done with teachers in Ontario who have had complaints made against them. Several news articles appeared in highly respected Ontario publications: <u>Why bad teachers don't get fired in Ontario</u> by Margaret Wente, Globe and Mail,

(2012), <u>Bad Teachers: Ontario's secret list</u> by Kevin Donovan, The Toronto Star, (2011), and <u>Why it's so hard to fire bad teachers </u>by Rachel Mendleson, Macleans Magazine, (2009), detailing shocking actions by teachers who were not fired, some not even disciplined. The issues included sexual behaviours, name-calling, threats or innuendos, and Principals and Vice Principals not reporting children's allegations of sexual abuse, as required (now) by law.

Children's voices are still often not listened to, so complaints made about abuse by a teacher are often ignored for years, or the teachers are transferred to other schools—just as the Catholic church has done with pedophile priests. The Supreme Court of B.C. has just approved a class-action lawsuit against two Catholic colleges by former students who allege they were abused by Christian Brothers who had been transferred there from a Newfoundland orphanage where rampant sexual and physical abuse occurred. (David Carrigg, Vancouver Sun, March 14, 2023)

Even today, students who see and report molestation by a teacher are often not believed. In Canada, Julie Ireton of the CBC reported (in a podcast called "The Band Played On" 2019), that, for more than thirty years, three teachers at Bell High School in Ottawa sexually abused dozens of teenaged boys and girls. Many of the students said that the music teacher "did it openly or locked the doors at recess or lunch hours." Nothing was done, despite concerns being raised by teachers and parents about two of the perpetrators. The school boards didn't call the police or carry out thorough investigations. So, though laws and attitudes toward child sexual abuse have changed substantially from the

1950s, dealing effectively with the molesters lags behind. Our situation in Leskard not only wasn't unique, but, as the Macleans article (Nov. 15, 2022) <u>A Monster in the Classroom</u> illustrates, a similar lack of care for children preyed on by sexual predators remains to this day.

The wide use of social media today is having an effect on dealing with the "inappropriate behaviour" of teachers, though. In only two days, more than five hundred and eighty people, including former and current students, signed an online petition requesting a teacher in Taber, Alberta, be fired. CBC News said (Feb. 25, 2021) that the "teacher has been removed from any student involvement following the … petition." The Horizon School Division said the "allegations are being investigated." In this case, students and parents bypassed the Board of Education, nor did they complain to the Principal—their grievances were made public. Perhaps people are just sick and tired of teachers getting away with the unthinkable regarding their children.

* * *

In January 2020, Thomas Grieve, a teacher in Whitby, Ontario, was convicted for "sexually touching students." He received two years less ten days, probation for thirty-five months, and a permanent place on the sex offenders list.

The description of Grieve's behaviour, his testimony and the testimony of his victims obtained from "Whitby This Week," (Mitchell 2019), revealed much that is backed up in the research about child molesters—and paralleled the situation at our school, over sixty years earlier.

First of all, Grieve, though convicted in 2020 on fifteen charges, had victimized children as far back as 2010. Our

Teacher molested girls from his earliest teaching days—and he taught in our school for at least twelve years.

In 2012, Grieve's actions with young girls in his care were so obvious, the principal at the elementary school Mr. Grieve taught at, warned him, "I have to advise you that these actions are completely unacceptable and cannot continue," and to stop or his "conduct with students might land him in trouble." (Whitby this Week June 18, 2019) His actions included "hugs, caresses, and stroking on various parts of their bodies." (Whitby this Week, June 18, 2019) Our Teacher's actions with female students were much the same and were discovered only a couple of years into his teaching career. Despite being found out, he didn't stop.

When he was on the witness stand, Mr. Grieve denied he'd ever touched a child for a sexual purpose, flatly refuting testimony by child witnesses who said he'd caressed and placed his hand under their clothing, or touched them on their buttocks and thighs." (Mitchell 2019) He touched children in the open environment of the classroom. (Mitchell 2019) Our Teacher also touched children underneath their clothes, sometimes in front of the class, put girls on his knee, and touched their legs.

The judge in the trial stated, "These children were in a safe environment—their school. That community was entitled to expect their children would be safe" (Mitchell 2020)—as was our community.

The judge also said he had received many letters of support from friends, family and colleagues of Grieve but noted, "Those who commit sexual assault often have a very positive background and antecedents," and added that, while such defendants "have the capacity to express remorse and empathy," he noted that Grieve "has not expressed even a murmur of remorse." Nor did our Teacher.

Grieve pleaded not guilty and said that his "tendency to initiate physical contact with students was misinterpreted by his accusers." This is consistent with what our Teacher had said.

On December 8th, 2020, "following a retroactive look through hundreds of discipline cases" of sexual misconduct, "the Ontario College of Teachers has officially revoked the licences of twenty-eight teachers, some from the past few years, others from cases ten or twenty years ago." (Donovan 2021) Many were no longer practicing teachers, according to the college. At least five were. While I celebrate this decision on the part of the College, it is long overdue, and says nothing about what will happen in future cases. And our Teacher still remains on the list of teachers with intact licences.

References:

Arabi, S. (2018). <u>Why do people believe narcissists rather than their victims?</u> Thought Catalogue.

Bala, Nicholas (1999) *Outline of Evidence*, Ministry of the Attorney General, jus.gov.on.ca

Bardon, Adrian, (2020). <u>Humans are hardwired to dismiss facts that don't fit their worldview.</u> The conversation.com

Bardon, Adrian (2020). *The Truth about Denial*, Oxford University Press, NY, NY

Barrett, Stanley R. (1994) *Paradise, Class, Commuters, and Ethnicity in Rural Ontario.* Toronto: University of Toronto Press.

De Becker, Gavin (1997) *The Gift of Fear.* Back Bay Books.

Donovan, K. (Sept. 29, 2011). <u>Bad teachers: Ontario's secret list</u>. The Star, Toronto.

Donovan, K. (Feb. 17, 2021). <u>Ontario College of Teachers names 28 teachers whose licenses have been revoked for sexual misconduct</u>. <u>www.Ca.news.yahoo.com/Ontario-college-teachers-names-28</u>

Filteau, J. (Feb. 23, 2004). <u>Understanding of child sex abuse has evolved in last 50 years</u>. Catholic News Service.

Gauthier-Duchesne, Amelie, Hebert, Martine, Daspe, Marie-Eve (2017). Gender as a Predictor of Posttraumatic Stress Symptoms and Externalizing Behaviour Problems in Sexually Abused Children. Child Abuse and Neglect, 64, 79-88.

Glenn, Amy W. (Dec. 14, 2018). Intuition is parents' greatest tool to fight child sexual abuse – and many won't use it. Philly Voice.

Gurnon, Emily. (Dec. 8, 2016) Childhood Trauma Effects Often Persist into 50s and Beyond. nextavenue.org.

Ireton, J. (2019). The Band Played On, Podcast, CBC Media Centre. https://www.cbc.ca/mediacentre/program/the-band-played-on

Kahn-Harris, Keith (2018). *Denial, the Unspeakable Truth*, Kendal, Cumbria: Notting Hill Editions.

Kehoe, J. (2018). Why visiting your ancestral home feels so familiar: It's literally in your bones. Matadornetwork.com.

Kristjanson, G. (2013). Predatory realms: To admire and desire the child in portal fantasy. Monsters and the Monstrous, Vol. 3, no.1, pp. 53-64.

Lowen, L. (Oct. 6, 2019). The cold hard facts on child sexual abuse. Thoughtco.com

Mendleson, R. (July 8, 2009). Why it's so hard to fire bad teachers. Macleans.

Mintz, Stephen (July 13, 2012) Placing childhood sexual abuse in historical perspective. Social Science Research Council

Mitchell, J. (June 25, 2019). Teacher on trial claims students misinterpreted his conduct. Durham Region.com.

Mitchell, J. (May 30, 2019). Child witness gives emotional testimony about touching by teacher. Durham Region.com.

Mitchell, J. (Jan. 7, 2020). Whitby Teacher sentenced to 2 years for sexually touching students. Whitby this Week.

Michell, J. (June 5, 2019). Whitby teacher went from 'cool' to 'creepy', sex assault trial hears. Durham Region. coNiem

Montaldo, Charles. (2019). Profile and common characteristics of a pedophile. Vietnam National University.

Mouallem, O. (Nov. 15, 2022) A monster in the classroom. Macleans Magazine Nov. 15, 2022.

National Association of Adult Survivors of Child Abuse, (2012). Articles 040512:

Grooming: How Child Molesters Create Willing Victims

Petrie, Anne. (1998) Gone to an Aunt's. McLelland & Stewart: Toronto.

Rosemond, John. (2013). Raising Kids in 1950s Households vs. Todays. Hartford Courant.

Rosner, Elizabeth. (2017) Survivor Café. The Legacy of Trauma and the Labyrinth of Memory. Counterpoint. Berkley, CA.

Science Daily. (2019) University of Michigan

Schmidt, Helen and Rutherford, Sidney, (1976). Out of the Mists, Printed by the Orono Weekly Times.

Shaw, Garfield (editor). (1980). Picture the Way We Were: A Pictorial History of Darlington and Clarke Townships. Published by Sam & Lois Adams, Patrick & Lynn Mothersill,

Stout, M. (2006). <u>The Sociopath Next Door</u>. Harmony Books: Random House.

Szalavitz, M. (27 Feb. 2018). <u>Why we're psychologically hardwired to blame the victim</u>. The Guardian.

Twomey, J. (27 January, 2017). <u>Don't tell, don't ask, don't listen: The trinity of ignoring childhood</u>. Wiley Periodicals Inc.

Wente, M. (June 12, 2012). <u>Why bad teachers don't get fired in Ontario</u>. Globe and Mail.

9 781990 496714